# THE SOUND OF ROMANCE

## LEGACY OF THE HEART BOOK 2

### DANICA FAVORITE

ISBN-paperback:

1945079045

9781945079047

Visit my website at www.danicafavorite.com

Printed in the United States of America

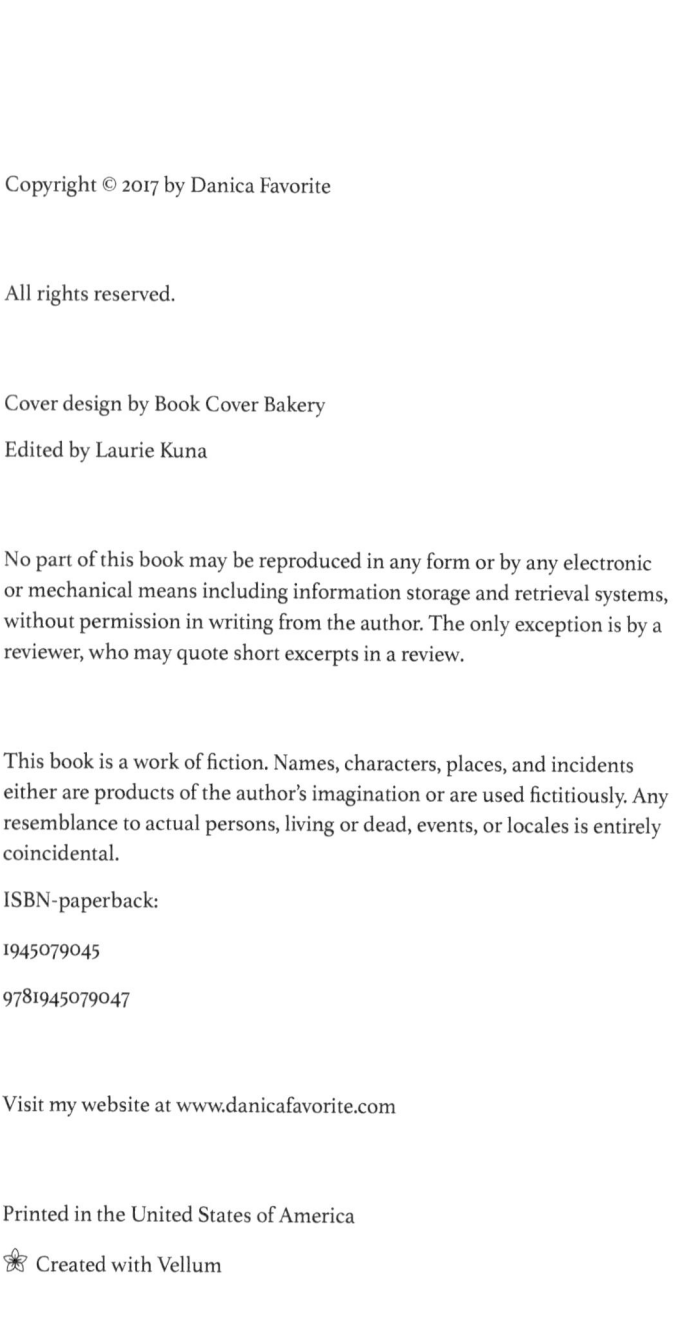 Created with Vellum

# 1

ole Anderson had been in love with Allie Bigby for just about ever. To some, it might sound like an exaggeration, but from the moment he laid eyes on her in elementary school, he knew that someday he was going to make Allie Bigby his wife. When he told his best friend Peter Houston, Peter had scoffed saying a third-grader would never waste his time on someone in a baby class, because Allie was a first-grader. But even then, Cole held firm to that belief. He'd just kept it to himself for all these years.

Except for a few failed attempts at getting her attention in high school, Cole had never let on how deeply he cared for Allie. He'd always hoped that someday, they'd find a way to be together. Which was hard to do when Allie never seemed to know he existed.

When he saw her working the register at Gas N' Shop, after him having been gone for more than ten years, his heart skipped a beat. No ring on the finger, and from what his sister-in-law had told him, no guy in the picture at all. He'd just hoped for a little more time before being faced with his childhood crush. Even so, he hadn't expected the memories of Allie to come to mind so readily.

"How can I help you?" Allie said with the dimpled smile he'd never been able to get out of his mind.

"I'm looking for..."

What had he come in there for? Cole looked around frantically. Gum? No. Mints? No. Dried beef sticks? No. Tacky Christmas knickknacks? No. Woman with a crying baby on the other side of the store? That triggered something.

"I need a wife," he blurted.

Allie gaped at him, just as she had in high school when his grand attempt at asking her to Homecoming had crashed and burned. He'd been certain that if she could see just how much he was willing to do for her, she'd realize what a great guy he was.

How was he supposed to know that singing "You've Lost That Loving Feeling" to a girl only resulted in a date in the movie, *Top Gun*? Maybe, if she'd been as airplane crazy as he'd been at the time, she'd have seen the old movie and known what to do. But that was beside the point.

Had he just told Allie Bigby that he was looking for a wife?

"I'm afraid we're fresh out of wives," she said, shaking her head. "Actually, I'm pretty sure we stopped selling females here about twenty years ago, when they converted the sale barn to the Gas N' Shop. And even then, I don't think they sold humans."

Was she trying to be funny or was she being serious? It was hard to tell with Allie because every time he tried to talk to her, everything he said came out so jumbled that she always walked away shaking her head. Like she was doing now.

"No, wait. I... that's not what I meant. I need something for my wife."

Oh no. He didn't have a wife. What was he saying? Why couldn't he string more than two words together in a sentence when he was around her?

"Sorry. I meant my brother's wife. Jess sent me. The..." He took a deep breath.

What was wrong with him? A simple errand for his sister-in-law and he couldn't remember what it was. Why did Allie Bigby make him so discombobulated? Recognition dawned on Allie's face.

"She was supposed to pick up some things from me earlier, is that what you mean?"

"Yes." Cole let out a long sigh. "I can't believe I forgot what it was. Some kind of salve she needed for the baby's diaper rash."

Diaper rash. One more inappropriate topic to be discussing with the woman of his dreams. But surely Allie knew what he was there for, and that it was meant for diaper rash. After all, Allie was the one who made the stuff. From what Jessica had told him, she was a real whiz at creating homemade items out of lavender.

"Cole Anderson." She said his name slowly as she shook her head. "I heard you were here for a visit."

"You remember me?"

Allie stared at him. "How could I not? You made high school miserable for me."

Yeah, so on the scale of one to ten of the world's greatest love stories, he was pretty sure this response wouldn't even give it a zero. He tried consoling himself by saying that at least she remembered him, but from the look on her face, he'd rather she didn't.

Could he get a do-over on this whole pursuing Allie thing?

"I'm sorry, I don't really remember that part." It was the best he could come up with on such short notice. Especially because he thought that he'd been the one humiliated, not Allie.

Allie gave him a smile that he didn't think she meant in a nice way.

"Oh, but I do. I know you supposedly had a crush on me back then, but you had some funny ways of showing a girl you liked her. So please, do me a favor. Steer clear of me while you're here." Allie reached under the counter and then handed him a box.

"Here's the salve. Take it and go before something terrible happens."

From the way she talked, Cole supposed he should have been grateful she didn't hand him a restraining order. It was slightly mortifying that his attempts at getting her to go out with him in high school were such a bad memory for her.

He'd envisioned that his reunion with Allie would be a little more... joyous. Or at least the same kind of reunion he'd had with his old friends when he ran into them since his return to Arcadia Valley. When he stopped by El Corazon, his favorite Mexican restaurant, he was immediately greeted by his old friend Javier, who'd given him dinner on the house because it had been so long since they'd seen each other.

Several of their other old friends had stopped in, and it was almost like a reunion. Allie's brother, Andrew, had also been one of Cole's good friends, and he'd come by. Though maybe Cole should have gotten the hint when he'd asked about Allie, and Andrew had abruptly changed the subject.

As Cole turned to leave, he nearly ran into a short

woman with dark hair, who clearly had something on her mind.

"I knew it!"

The woman yanked the box out of Cole's hand, and held it in the air. "You *are* selling your lavender stuff out of here. Just wait until I tell Dan."

As she was speaking, the door had opened and an older, balding man stepped in. "Tell me what?"

"Even though you've asked her not to, Allie has been selling her lavender products here at the Gas N' Shop. I just watched this man get some from her."

Cole glanced over at Allie, who looked even more angry than she had when she'd talked to him.

"I didn't sell anything," Allie said. "No money changed hands. You can check the security camera if you don't believe me."

At least Cole had a chance to help her out of this mess. "It's true. I didn't give her any money. I was just picking this up for my sister-in-law. She already paid for it."

Instead of looking grateful, Allie looked like she wanted to throttle him.

"That's still selling," the woman said, smiling like she'd won a big prize.

"I didn't sell it to her." Allie turned to Dan. "It was just a favor to a friend. A gift. How many times have you left things here for friends to pick up? Just the other day, you had me give those flies you made to Stan Baumgardner. I made the salve for Jess, but I didn't have time to drop it off at her house earlier. I was going to run it to her when I got off," Allie looked over at the clock on the wall. "Which was supposed to be fifteen minutes ago."

Dan nodded slowly. "Who is this guy, then?"

Allie gave him a look, like she wanted him to stay out of

it. "Her brother-in-law. I don't know why she sent him, but it doesn't really matter. The point is, it was just something I made for her friend, who sent someone to pick it up rather than wait for me to come by."

"But you're still wasting company time," the nasty woman said, crossing her arms over her chest. "I'll bet you don't have those reports done."

"Actually, I do." Allie walked back around the counter and pulled out a folder from underneath. "I have all the stocking done for the day, and I went through the order list and updated it, and-"

"Enough," Dan said. "I get the picture. But you know how I feel about you conducting personal business from the store."

Shaking her head, Allie let out a long sigh. "I do. Honestly, since the last time you talked to me about this, I haven't brought my work here. This was just a favor for a friend whose baby has a miserable diaper rash. It was an emergency."

"Emergency or not, friends are still personal business," the woman said.

Cole wanted to smack the smirk off her face. Why wasn't Allie defending herself more strongly? If she wouldn't, then he would. He turned to her. "I know it's hard for you to understand what it must be like to have friends, but you should give Allie a break. She's the nicest person I know, and she doesn't deserve to be talked to like this."

"It's fine, Cole. Just go home, and I'll sort this out. Nadia just misunderstood what was going on, and that's that. But as she has rightfully pointed out, this is a place of business, and we all need to get back to work."

Allie turned to go back to the counter, but Nadia stopped

her. "I'm here now, you can just go home. We'll call you if we decide you can come back to work."

"What are you saying?" Allie's voice was quiet, and Cole hated the defeated tone it had taken.

Surely they weren't going to fire her over something so silly?

Cole took another step forward. "You can't just leave her hanging like that. You haven't given her due process, and if you're going to fire her, then you need to give her her last paycheck."

Nadia nodded, and for the first time, she looked almost like she was going to be reasonable. "You're right. Let me go into the back and write her a check. That way she knows for sure she's fired."

That wasn't exactly what he'd been aiming for, especially since Allie looked like she was about to cry. But really, was working for such an awful person the best she could do with her life?

"It's a terrible job anyway," Cole said. "Allie doesn't need this job."

Allie shot him a glare that made him want to be sick. Apparently, defending her had not been his brightest idea.

"Actually, I do need this job. It's a great job, and I'm happy to have it. Cole doesn't speak for me, just as you don't speak for Dan. He owns the place, not you."

Turning to Dan, Allie said, "You know I'm a good worker. I come in early, I stay late, I cover whatever shifts you need. Yes, I made a mistake, and I'm sorry. It didn't cost us any business, since no customers have come in this entire space of time. I can assure you, it won't happen again."

At least Dan looked like he was thinking about her words. He nodded slowly, as if she had made several good points. And Cole would admit that she had. Probably better points than he had. He should have done what Allie asked, and stayed out of it.

"How many times has she said that?" Nadia said, glaring at Dan. "You promoted me to assistant manager to make this store more profitable. She's a distraction from where this business needs to go. This isn't the first time we've had to talk to her about her many failings. If you can't man up and do the right thing, then you're going to need to find another assistant manager."

Was this woman serious?

Apparently, she was. Because Dan looked completely and utterly defeated. "I'm sorry, Allie."

Allie nodded slowly. "I know you are." Then she looked over Nadia and shook her head. "It didn't have to be like this. I really wish we could have worked together in a cooperative manner for the good of our community. I'm sorry you didn't feel the same way."

Her words didn't appear to affect Nadia at all. "I'll just go get your check."

"Thanks." Then Allie turned to Dan. "I hope you know what you're doing, because you and I both know this isn't right."

He didn't respond, and Cole was glad. Mostly because Cole wasn't sure he could continue keeping his mouth shut in light of this injustice.

Still, he had to say something to encourage her. "It'll be all right. You'll find a new job. A better job."

Allie spun and glared at him. "Since apparently, I no longer work here, I also no longer have to be nice to the customers. I know you think you mean well, but you've done enough damage. If you want to help me, do as I asked and go home. And never bother me again."

As reunions went, this definitely was not what Cole had been expecting.

Coming back to Arcadia Valley was only supposed to be a temporary pit stop over the holidays until Cole could figure out what he wanted to do with his life now that the Army had determined he was unfit for service. Thanks to a training jump gone wrong, his back was too messed up for him to pass his physicals.

For a brief moment, he'd actually thought that maybe he could find a way to start over in Arcadia Valley. His brother, his uncle, old friends, and seeing Allie again. He hadn't been able to win her heart in high school, and now, that goal seemed farther away than ever.

Maybe it was a sign that he really and truly did have to move on.

His life was basically ruined. And judging by the way she'd glared at him on his way out, she thought hers was too. The difference was, somebody as pretty, healthy, smart, and talented as Allie had a lot of options. No one grew up wanting to work at the Gas N' Shop.

He really had been trying to help. But maybe, this was all a blessing in disguise. He'd help Allie find a better job, and hopefully, in the process, figure out his own life as well.

## 2

C ole Anderson. Jess had told her he was in town, but Allie had never expected him to show up at the store. She'd told Jess not to send Cole to pick up the salve. Allie had even volunteered to deliver it on her way home since she hadn't had time to do it on her way to work. Jess had very kindly told her that wasn't necessary and she would be there to take care of it herself. Jess might be Allie's best friend, but this was not the action of a so-called best friend.

Jess hadn't gone to high school with them, so she wasn't aware of all the horrible things Cole had done to ruin Allie's life. So perhaps Jess's oversight could be chalked up to not realizing the severity of the situation. Bad things happened when Cole and Allie were in the same room.

As Allie gathered her things while waiting for her check, she looked around the Gas N' Shop. She'd worked here off and on since high school, and she loved this place, even if it wasn't the most glamorous job in town.

Dan scurried back into the main store from the back like

the rat that he was. Why didn't he have any backbone when it came to Nadia?

"I'm sorry," Dan said awkwardly, like he hadn't already said it a dozen times. If he was sorry, why was he letting this farce continue?

"There's still time to do the right thing," she told him, knowing he wouldn't, but feeling like she had to try anyway.

Why did Cole have to butt in like that? If he hadn't insulted Nadia, Allie would probably still have a job. And then for him to insult this job?

She would cry, except crying never solved anything, and she wasn't about to give Nadia the satisfaction of knowing she'd won.

Because she hadn't.

All right. She had. Nadia had been trying to push Allie out ever since she showed up in town the year before, and no matter how hard Allie had worked to be nice to her, Nadia always turned it into some weird petty fight.

But why, with the holidays and her brother's wedding coming, did this have to happen now?

Nadia waltzed back in like she'd won Queen of the County Fair or some other nonsense. "Here's your check. I docked you an hour for wasting company time today."

"You know it didn't take an hour."

"So, sue me," Nadia said, grinning because she knew Allie would do no such thing. Allie's cousin Caroline was married to a lawyer and wouldn't mind helping her. But for ten bucks? It wasn't worth the effort.

"Don't worry about it," she said. "Consider it my Christmas gift to you. Especially since you had me scheduled to work both Christmas Eve and Christmas day, and now you're going to have to find someone to fill those shifts."

It felt good to score that point, especially as she watched

the panicked looks on both Nadia's and Dan's face. They knew that she always worked the holidays because most of the other employees had kids, and she didn't think it was right to take a parent from a child on a holiday.

Emily Locke, who was supposed to take over for her at the end of her shift, breezed in. "Hey, Allie."

"If only you'd been five minutes early for a change, instead of thirty-five minutes late," Allie muttered.

"Oh, sorry, did you have someplace to be?" Emily looked genuinely sad that she'd put her out. "You should've told me. I would've gotten here sooner."

Then Emily stopped. "Oh. I didn't realize Nadia and Dan were here. I... um..."

Emily had been written up countless times for being late, and Allie felt bad for pointing it out. The last thing she needed was for her bad mood to ruin someone else's life.

"It's all right," Nadia said, sounding a little too sickeningly sweet. "You can make up for it by working Christmas."

The horrified look on Emily's face made Allie feel awful. "But... my kids. Allie always works Christmas."

Allie patted Emily's hand. "You missed the big show. Nadia finally got what she wanted and fired me."

"What I wanted?" Nadia made a noise. "It isn't my fault you broke company rules, were insubordinate, and have continued the inappropriate behavior I've discussed with you many times. You should be lucky you kept your job this long."

Nadia sounded like she'd been reading from a human resources manual. The trouble was, every infraction Nadia listed was manufactured, and she knew it.

"I don't understand. I don't know what any of those things mean, but I do know that Allie is the backbone of this place. She's always there for us. What are we going to do without her?"

Emily looked at Dan as she made her plea. Though the other girl's words were humbling, and it felt good to be so recognized, it seemed to only increase the fury on Nadia's face.

"Actually run a business," Nadia said. "And if you don't shape up, you'll be joining her in the unemployment line. We have far too many workers who don't follow the rules and are a drain on our resources. We can't afford to keep giving so many chances."

It was tempting to remind Nadia that the kind of worker she seemed to want didn't exist in Arcadia Valley. Gas N' Shop didn't pay well enough for many people to stay long. And, now that Nadia was running the show, most people didn't want to deal with her negative attitude. Based on what she saw from her coworkers, and the amount of work they did, she did the work of three people. Nadia was going to have a hard time replacing her, but that was her problem.

However, she did feel obligated to help Emily. As Allie had told Cole, this was a job, and the people who worked here needed that job.

"Emily is a good worker, and you know that. This is about whatever personal problem you have with me. Don't take it out on her." Allie turned to Emily and gave her a smile. "Don't worry about your kids. If you can't find someone to take your shift, I'll watch them. A holiday on the farm will be a treat for them."

Emily nodded slowly, like she was afraid to speak for fear of further angering Nadia.

"I guess I should be going," Allie said. She looked directly at Dan, then shook her head. "I hope you know what you're doing. I've always been there for you, always been there for the store and the people who work here."

Tears tickled the backs of her eyes, so she grabbed her bag and walked out. Stupid Cole Anderson. In high school, it had only been Allie's life that he ruined. But now, a lot more people had been hurt because of his insane obsession with her. Though it was easy to just blame Cole, someone else had a hand in this nightmare.

Once she got to her car, she dialed Jess's number, grateful for her Bluetooth system.

"I was just wondering about you," Jess said, the smile evident in her voice. "Cole hasn't returned home yet, so I'm hoping this is a good sign."

"You thought wrong. He came into the Gas N' Shop, asking for a wife. Which would have almost been something I could have laughed off, but then he got me fired."

When Jess didn't respond right away, Allie continued. "I know you mean well, and I know you think Cole and I would be absolutely perfect together. But like I told you, we have history. There will be no happily-ever-after for me and Cole. If there's something that mixes less well than oil and water, that would be us. Please don't try to fix us up again. And please, don't send him on any errands that involve me. If you need something from me, then take care of it yourself."

After brief moment, Jess said, "I'm sorry. I guess I didn't realize it was that bad."

Hearing the hurt in her best friend's voice only made the situation worse. Jess had meant well, but she didn't understand.

"Wait, what? What do you mean he got you fired?"

Allie sighed. It wasn't entirely Cole's fault, but he'd sure made the situation worse.

"Nadia walked in as Cole was leaving with the salve. She saw it and threw a fit because she interpreted it as me selling my lavender goods from the Gas N' Shop. I tried explaining the situation, but you know how Nadia is. And then Cole jumped into it and completely insulted Nadia, which sent her over the edge, so she fired me."

At Jess's matching sigh, Allie felt even worse.

"This is all my fault," Jess said. "I just thought that maybe if you guys saw each other again after all these years, whatever happened between you in the past would be different, and you would fall in love, get married, and then we could really be sisters. I'd forgotten that Nadia had it out for you."

Allie turned onto the main road, wishing she hadn't called Jess, even though she would have eventually found out. She hadn't meant to burden her friend.

"It's not your fault. Technically, Nadia was right in that I had been asked not to sell any of my lavender products at the store. I tried to argue that I wasn't selling anything, because I made this for you as a gift. But I underestimated just how much Nadia hates me. I just wish I knew why."

"I know it won't make much of a difference, but I'll pay you for the salve if you want."

Jess's offer was sweet, but Allie wasn't going to take money from her friend.

"No. At least now I can hold up my head knowing that I really hadn't done anything wrong. If I take your money, then it will be a product I sold, and that makes Nadia right. So it's what I told you it was going to be when we talked this morning. Something I'm doing for you because you're my friend."

Maybe it was stupid for her to turn down the money, considering Nadia had shorted her check, and she no longer had a job. But her principles were worth more than money, something her family would probably disagree with, at least her parents would. But that was a battle she had been fighting for a long time.

"Is it too soon to suggest that this might be a blessing in disguise? You've been working too much to really get your lavender business going. Maybe this is your chance to finally get off the ground and be a success."

Though Allie typically appreciated her friend's positive attitude, now was definitely not the time to suggest such a thing.

"My business takes capital, capital provided by the wages I earn at my job. No job, no capital."

Of course, if people would pay her all the money they owed her for her lavender goods, that would bring in a little more of the money she needed. But most of the boutiques and shops that carried her products operated on a consignment basis and were notoriously slow for sending payments to her. Andrew was good at managing these things, since finances were not her strong suit, but now that he had gone back to school and was getting ready for his wedding, he'd given a lot of those responsibilities back to her. So, she just worked more hours at the Gas N' Shop, hoping to be able to cover all her expenses. Without her job... Allie sighed.

She'd just have to find another one, that's all.

"I didn't realize, I'm sorry," Jess said.

And now Allie was the one who was sorry. She hadn't meant to make her best friend feel bad. Her only intention had been to get Jess to end her stupid fantasy about Allie and Cole ending up together.

"I know. And it's okay, really. You meant well. Unfortunately, you didn't understand the power of how badly Cole ruins things for me. Every horrible thing that happened to me in high school was either directly or indirectly Cole's fault."

She thought she'd done a good job of trying to forgive him, but forgiving someone was a lot easier when that person was thousands of miles away, and you never had to see them again.

"I'm really sorry," Jess said. "It seemed like everyone laughed about the stories, even you. I didn't realize that you were genuinely hurt."

That one was on Allie. She should have spoken up more to let people know that she didn't think any of those stories were funny. Not when she'd been the butt of the joke.

"I got sick of everyone telling me I was being a big crybaby. The few times I complained to the staff at the school, they acted like I was the one who was the problem because what Cole had done was so cute and adorable. Even Andrew. He's always been there for me, but since Andrew was Cole's friend, Andrew always acted like I was overreacting. He kept telling me that I just needed to give him a chance. He's always told me what a great guy he is. Maybe he is a great guy. Just not the guy for me. So, if you wouldn't mind, could you please just leave it alone? Things are really stressful for me right now, and I can't have more Cole drama to deal with."

It was Allie's usual litany of problems, but with adding Cole into the mix, and now not having a job, she wasn't sure she had the strength. Jess would tell her to come over, they'd have a cup of tea, and somehow, she would have the strength to face the craziness at Bigby Farm.

"I'd invite you to come over here, but with Cole probably on his way back, I imagine it would be pretty awkward."

Allie hated the resignation in Jess's voice. They always

spent a lot of time together, and just when she needed it most, Jess was too busy with Cole to spend time with her.

But that wasn't really Cole's fault.

Even in blaming him for all the things that had gone wrong, she knew that he'd never intended her any harm. Like the time he'd almost gotten her suspended from school for cheating. Which she hadn't done, but she'd been in the wrong place at the wrong time, and Cole, in trying to help her, made it look like she had been involved. It had taken Gram, shaking down the parents of the kids who had been involved and getting them to admit that Allie was an innocent bystander, to get Allie out of trouble.

Only this time, Gram wasn't going to be able to save her, and she would admit that she was partially at fault in this situation because she hadn't realized the depth of Nadia's desire to get rid of her.

Which meant she couldn't really even be mad at Jess. She, too, meant well, but it seemed like everyone's good intentions toward Allie always seemed to backfire.

"It's fine," Allie said. "I'm sure as soon as Andrew learns Cole is back in town, he'll want Cole to come over so they can catch up. I'll talk to him and see if he can give me warning, and on that date, I'll come to your house."

"You're really going to try to hide from Cole the whole time he's here?"

The way she said it made her feel almost childish. But she was almost at a breaking point. A few snow flurries hit her windshield, reminding her that she still had to go pay the heat bill for the farm and drop off the rest of the payments for her bills in the mail.

Allie sighed as she glanced at the bill. Andrew had told her to come to him if she needed help, but with everything he had on his plate, it seemed selfish for her to bother him.

She had enough money in her account to take care of it. And if she stretched the remaining money, plus this last paycheck, maybe she could make it all work until one of the boutiques finally paid her.

There was no way she could handle Cole on top of all this.

"Avoiding him might not be the most mature answer, but I don't think anyone understands what I'm going through right now. It's like everything bad in my life that I've tried to push away so I can move on and be happy is confronting me all at once. If I can avoid one of the things that makes me crazy so I have the energy to deal with something else that makes me crazy, then I think it's for the best."

Jess made a sympathetic noise, and even though she didn't know the extent of Allie's problems, it felt like she had someone in her corner. "I hadn't thought of it that way. I promise there will be no more meddling in hopes of getting you and Cole together. I'm really sorry I tried to do so in the first place."

Before she could respond, she noticed that the car in front of her had stopped. She pushed her foot into the brake as hard as she could, but even before the crunch of metal on metal, she knew she'd been too late. In her short drive from the store to her house, the roads had gotten icy, too icy to make a quick stop.

Even though Cole hadn't caused this accident, the first thought in her mind was him. If she hadn't been so distracted, trying to explain about him to Jess, this accident never would've happened. She closed her eyes and said a little prayer that whoever she'd hit wasn't injured. It should have been her first thought, but God was just one more area of her life totally out of balance.

"Allie? Are you okay? It sounded like —"

"I hit someone." Tears filled her eyes. It wasn't Cole's fault that she'd done so. It was her fault, for not being able to control her emotions and her emotional responses to someone so that she wasn't too distracted to drive.

"Do you want me to call the police?"

"No. I'll let you go. I can do it. I guess I've ruined my perfect driving record." Just as she was about to hit the button to end the call, a sickening feeling washed over her. She hadn't just hit some random person.

"I just hit Cole Anderson."

## 3

———

Cole jumped out of his truck and ran toward the other vehicle. He was fine, he just hoped that the person who'd hit him was as well. The roads had started to get icy, and he'd stopped too suddenly. He'd been trying to avoid hitting someone's dog, since after his interaction with Allie, he couldn't bear the thought of also killing someone's beloved pet. In a way, that's how he felt about what he'd done to her.

When he approached the other car, Cole's stomach sank. Of course, it would have to be Allie. Why would he have imagined any easier outcome?

When he got to her car, she was sitting in the driver seat, hands on the wheel, head rested against it. How badly was she hurt?

He pulled out his phone to call 911, and then she lifted her head. Tears were streaming down her cheeks as she opened the door. Maybe the only thing hurt was her pride.

If he called the police, she'd probably get the ticket. Even though he'd been the one to stop suddenly, the officer would say she'd been going too fast or following too closely. Something in him knew this was also his fault.

The way her car was crunched up, fixing the damage would be expensive. Fortunately, his old pickup truck was built like a beast. Practically indestructible. It had been his dad's truck before he'd gone off to the remote jungles to be a missionary. When his dad died, Uncle Vince told him that it was his. His brother had gotten their father's old Jeep, which he still had. When Cole had gone into the Army, his brother told him he'd keep the truck for him just in case he wanted it back again someday. Even though he'd always kind of thought it foolish to keep the vehicle, he was now grateful that it wasn't some rental car that had gotten bashed up. That would only complicate matters even more.

"Go ahead," she said, getting out of the car. "Gloat. I know I deserve it for how I treated you."

He hated that she blamed herself for the situation. In a way, it almost made him feel worse. She was a nice person, always had been. It was why she'd always been so irresistible to him. It seemed like whenever she was around, she did her best to make sure others felt good and confident. If there was a kid sitting alone, she'd sit by that child. If someone needed help, she would go out of her way to help them.

Which was why today's interaction at the Gas N' Shop had surprised him so much. Especially since that woman, Nadia, had been so bent on punishing Allie for what seemed like an innocent mistake. And then for her to shut him down so hard, well, he supposed he had it coming. It just wasn't like her to be so forceful.

"It wasn't your fault, it was just an accident. Accidents happen sometimes, it's just how life goes." He tried to sound reassuring, but she looked at him with such a forlorn expression that all Cole wanted to do was make it better for her.

"That's sweet of you to say, but I know I wasn't paying attention. I was distracted. I just wish it didn't have to happen now. It doesn't matter that my driving record is clean. I've never had a ticket. Never had an accident. But as soon as I go home, all I'm going to hear about is what a disappointment I am. It's one more way I can't be responsible. Now that Andrew is back in our parents' good graces, it's going to be once again, 'Why can't you be more like your brother Andrew? When are you going to have your life together? Why did you have to go and do a stupid thing like rear-ended someone? And oh, yeah, you can't even keep a job.'"

She shook her head at him, then started to cry. Cole started to lean into her to give her a hug, then he realized this was Allie, the woman who hated him.

"But are *you* all right? The important thing is that you're not injured. You're not, are you?"

She shook her head. "No. At least I have that going for me."

Then she straightened and gave him another look that reminded him of an injured puppy. "I'm sorry, I don't know what's gotten into me. I'm usually not such a downer. I just feel like everything is going wrong in my life all at once, and I'm powerless to stop it."

Then she looked up at the sky and said, "God, why? Did I do something wrong? I understand that bad things happen sometimes to help us grow, but don't you think this is a little too much growth all at once?"

She turned back to Cole. "Now you know I'm really crazy. Aren't you glad I never went out with you?"

He wanted to tell her that, crazy or not, he still would've

gone out with her. But given the fact that she'd made her lack of feelings for him clear, he didn't think that was the best option.

Instead, he said, "I don't know about that. I always thought you were a good person, and I can't imagine that's changed all that much. Let me call my brother, and he can give you a tow. I don't think your car is drivable."

Allie nodded slowly. "Shouldn't we call the police? You'll want for the accident report for your insurance, and I'm sure I probably deserve a ticket."

With everything she'd just said to him, even if Cole had wanted to call the police, he couldn't. "I don't see any reason to. My truck isn't damaged, so I'm not going to make a claim. I think you know my brother has his own garage. Let's see what it'll take to repair your car."

She looked even more glum. "I know. He does great work. He'd be my first choice, but there's no way I can pay for it on my own. I have full coverage on my car, so I'll figure out how to pay the deductible and it'll cover the rest."

Her family had never had money, and was it sad for Cole to see that she was still plagued by financial worries. He knew from Jess that she was starting her own business with her lavender products, but it hadn't occurred to him that money would be so tight. Then again, he'd just witnessed her getting fired from her job. A job she'd said she needed.

A sinking feeling hit his stomach. He hadn't just witnessed her getting fired. He'd been a part of the situation. Even though he'd only been trying to help, he couldn't help feeling like it was his fault.

He owed it to Allie to help her now.

"Why don't we wait and see what it will cost? As a friend of the family, I'm sure James would be willing to work out an arrangement."

"I wouldn't want to take advantage of him like that. Especially now that Jess is pregnant again. They need the money for the baby. It's just me. I'll call my customers and see if I can get payment, and hopefully, in a few weeks, I'll have the deductible covered." Allie picked up her phone, but Cole held out his hand.

"Please don't. I know you want to do the right thing, but I one hundred percent believe that this is partially my fault and I hate to see you suffer when I'm the one who has you so upset. If there's a new baby coming–"

Wait. He stared at her. His brother hadn't said anything about another baby. Caitlin was only six months old "Are you sure they're having another baby? If they were expecting again, James would've told me."

She slapped a hand over her mouth. Then she shook her head slowly, and moved her hand from her mouth, and said, "And it just keeps getting worse. If you want to do anything to help me, please don't tell your brother. Jess just found out, and she's trying to figure out how she's going to tell him. This wasn't planned, and she's not sure how he's going to react."

"It's a baby. I'm sure he'll be very happy." His words didn't seem to change the worried expression on her face. "But I can see where Jess would want to tell him and not have me sticking my nose into it. I promise I'll keep it a secret until he shares the news. And I'll act surprised. I don't understand why she told you first and not him. Shouldn't a wife tell her husband first?"

"In ideal circumstances, yes. Jess was complaining to me about how she hadn't been feeling well, and the way she described her symptoms, it sounded a lot like when she was pregnant with Caitlin. I suggested it to her, but she told me no, not only was she nursing, but they were being careful. It was so inconceivable to her that she could be pregnant, that I went out and bought the test. I made her take it, and it came out positive. I think it's going to take her a while to process the news, and I feel really terrible for saying something to you."

Once again, she looked like she was about to cry. In all the years he'd known Allie, he'd never seen her cry. Which made this whole situation seemed all the more unfortunate.

"I just don't know what's wrong with me these days," she said. "I would never spill a friend's secrets, and here I've just done so on a big one. I know you promised you wouldn't tell, but it doesn't erase the fact that I feel like a horrible person for it. And then there are all the horrible things I said to you, plus the fact that I've just hit you, and I have to go home with a broken car and pretend everything is all right when it isn't. Worse, I'm going to have to listen to the lecture on how poor Allie just can't get herself together."

When Cole had known Allie in high school, she'd been a smart, confident girl. She'd never seemed to care what anyone thought, which was what had inspired Cole to do what he thought was right. What had happened to Allie after all these years? Had he just not known her as well as he thought he did? Had he been silly for harboring feelings for her?

He looked at her and felt a resounding, "No!", deep within his soul. She might say her life was a mess, and some people might think that about her, but he could still see the Allie he'd first fallen in love with. And maybe, just like the day had not gone as he'd planned for himself, she was having the same day. And maybe, rather than them both letting it get to them, they could join forces to make it better.

"It sounds like you're having as rough of a time of I am," he said. "I don't know what gossip has gotten back to you or not, but my life is falling apart too. We got off on the wrong foot today, and everything just seems to be getting worse. But I think we could both use a friend right now, so can we have a do-over? I'm calling my brother and asking him to bring the tow truck. He'll look at your car and see what it'll take to fix it. I grew up helping him work on cars, so rather than being a burden on him, I'll lend a hand. We're not calling the police, we're not calling the insurance company. We can work it out between us because that's what friends should do."

Allie looked at him suspiciously.

"But we were never friends. Don't you remember?" She shook her head. "No, I guess you don't. You came in acting like the old times were good times."

Cole let out a long sigh. It seemed the past between them was so complicated, and all he wanted to do was make things right for them in the present. But how was he supposed to do that when they both had different remembrances of what things had been like?

"I think our past is something too complicated to resolve right here on the side of the road. But if you're willing, we'll get this taken care of, and maybe, in the coming weeks, we can work through that old stuff too. I'm sorry if all those things back then hurt you. I'd like to find a way to repair the damage. I don't expect your forgiveness overnight, but would you be willing for me to help you out?"

# 4

Had Cole always been this nice? Allie wasn't sure, but realizing how hard he was trying to make things right with her, even to the point of not reporting the accident, she had to say that she'd either misjudged him, or that maybe after all that time in the Army, Cole had grown up.

Not that it totally excused his role in her getting fired, but as part of the work she'd done in forgiving him in the past, she'd had to acknowledge that he'd never meant her any harm. Once again, she'd have to keep reminding herself of that fact.

It seemed like Cole was doing everything he could to be nice to her. Allie often felt like that was a rare occurrence in her world these days. Even though she got along with her brother and cousin and their significant others, and even Gram, it just seemed like the whole rest of the world was against her.

What a crazy world she lived in that her worst enemy, or at least the person she thought was her worst enemy, was the one being kind to her when she needed it the most.

"Okay," she said. "We'll do it your way. But you have to promise that you'll tell me if helping is a burden. I don't want to add to anyone else's problems."

She liked the way he looked at her then. Full of compassion and more. It wasn't that her brother and cousin didn't show those things to her. They did. They were just so busy with all of their stuff that she hated to burden them with hers. Odd that Allie, who never opened up to anyone, had shared so much with Cole. While it was one of the weirdest things in the world, it had seemed so natural.

"Sorry if I seem like such a mess," she said. "I'm usually much more in control of myself."

Cole's smile warmed her as he typed something into his phone, and seemed to get an immediate response. "My brother is on his way. You have to stop apologizing," he said. "It's okay to fall apart at times. Like I said, things haven't been going so great in my life either."

Once again, his words shamed Allie. She hadn't asked about what was going on in his life. She'd intentionally shut information about him out and knew little to nothing about him. Just that he was home on leave from the Army for a couple of weeks. She'd been wrong to do so. Hopefully, she would get the chance to rectify her mistake.

"I'm sorry things have been rough for you. Care to talk about it?"

Cole shrugged. Now that she was actually looking at him, she realized that he was kind of cute. Had he always been good-looking, or was he one of the guys who had been weird-looking in high school but over the years had become more handsome? She had to admit that she never really looked at him before. She'd never taken the time to see anything other than the fact that he annoyed her.

Maybe she was more in the wrong in this situation than she'd thought.

"I suppose, while we wait I can tell you," he said. "It's not like it's a big secret. And who knows, maybe you'll have a perspective different from everyone else's." He gestured to his truck. "Why don't we go sit while we wait for my brother to get here?"

"Sounds good. I can't believe you still have the same truck you drove in high school."

He looked surprised. "I would think you'd have no idea what I drove in high school. Considering your words earlier, and how oblivious you always seemed to act towards me."

Even though he had already suggested a forgive-and-forget type of approach, she was still embarrassed by his words. Was she that kind of monster? No, she wasn't a monster. But obviously, there was still a lot for her and Cole to work out between them.

"Of course, I knew the car you drove. I needed to know which cars to avoid. You lived just down the road. I learned to be very good about hiding from you. Especially when you went to see my brother. If I saw that truck pull into the driveway, I would always find a place to hide."

At Cole's pained expression, Allie sighed. "Sorry, that probably stung a little. My trouble with being honest is that sometimes maybe I can be a little too honest. I know I need to work on tempering it with kindness, but I couldn't think of how to do so in this circumstance. I guess what I should've said is that your car is pretty famous. After all, even in high school it was old. My brother and his friends all thought it was pretty cool."

Allie smiled at him, hoping to erase the still-troubled look on his face. Who would have thought that she'd be the one trying to comfort the person who'd tormented her all these years? "I realize that to guys, this is a sacrilege, but to me it's just a way to get from point A to point B. I don't even care if my car is cool or not, as long as it runs."

Cole finally smiled back at her. "Not everyone is a car person. Even Jess's eyes get glazed over when my brother and I are talking cars. For us, though, these are more than just vehicles. I'm not sure how much of my past you know, but they're part of our family history. After our parents died, Uncle Vince helped us fix them up, saying that we can at least have this one thing of our father's. He also thought it was a good idea for us to know how to work on our own cars, which is a skill a lot of people don't have. And in my opinion, extremely useful. After all, we can do most of the work on our cars ourselves. It's a living for my brother."

She remembered the story about the Anderson boys and their missionary parents dying when they were young. Jess had mentioned it several times about her husband, but until now, she hadn't made the connection with Cole. How had she been so close-minded towards him all these years?

He looked thoughtful for a moment, then he said, "This may sound stupid, but having my dad's old truck makes me feel close to him even though he's gone. As a teenager, I would drive around pretending I was talking to him."

Maybe some people would think it sounded weird, but Allie understood. Not the pretending he was talking to his dad part, but the idea that talking out loud to work through a problem could be beneficial. She talked to herself all the time, and while she supposed some people thought it was insane, it always made her feel good.

"I understand. Plenty of people think I'm crazy, and I don't have the excuse of a dead dad."

Cole grinned, like something good was passing between them. In the past, she'd always thought the way he looked at her and smiled was creepy. But now, she was comforted by this small gesture. Like she wasn't so alone.

Then he looked thoughtful. "No, but your dad wasn't really here, was he?"

Allie stilled. True, she didn't have a great relationship with her parents, but it felt weird to hear Cole remark on it. She stared at him for a moment, then he reached out and took her hand.

"I'm sorry. I didn't mean to sound like I was being insensitive. Maybe you didn't have the same feelings about him as Andrew, sorry for assuming. I just remember when your father was offered that job in Spokane, then Seattle, it had really hurt Andrew that he'd chose to move and let you guys stay here."

Ordinarily, she would have jerked her hand away. It bothered her when guys were presumptuous and grabby. That wasn't what he seemed to be doing, though. He was offering genuine comfort over something she'd said was a difficult subject. Once again, she was struck by how she'd underestimated him. She squeezed his hand, then gently pulled it away so she didn't seem like she was being rude.

"I understand. I apologize if I seemed a little jumpy. People just assume things about our family, and it drives me crazy. I suppose that's what I thought you were doing. I'd forgotten that you and Andrew were good friends."

For a long time, she'd been angry at her brother for remaining friends with the boy who'd tormented her through high school. But now, as she saw the genuine compassion on Cole's face, she realized that he'd probably understood a lot of Andrew's problems, and had been there for her brother.

"My father wasn't dead," Allie continued. "But you're right. He was gone. However, he was constantly calling and weighing in about how he thought we should run our lives. I know Andrew feels like he got the bulk of it, but all I ever heard was what a disappointment I was, and why couldn't I be more like my brother. He says it was no picnic for him either, but what I wouldn't have given to have our father say one nice thing to me. I feel kind of ridiculous for resenting it now, because you probably wish you could've just heard your father say anything."

Cole gave her a look of understanding. Like he was a real friend. "Andrew and I got in a fight about that once. He was complaining about your father, and I got mad and told him that at least he had a father. I thought about it over the years, and how I was wrong to say that. Thanks for reminding me. I've been wanting to tell him, because I want to make things right."

A tow truck came toward them, and Allie immediately recognized it as being James's. She was almost disappointed he had arrived. She always thought conversation with Cole Anderson would be the worst thing ever, but Allie couldn't think of a conversation she'd had lately that she'd enjoyed more. He was a good listener, but he was also understanding and thoughtful in his responses. It seemed almost a shame she had spent all of these years being his enemy.

# 5

J ess was waiting expectantly when they arrived at the Anderson farm. Allie was pretty sure her friend was checking to make sure no blood had been shed. Hopefully she wouldn't gloat too much when she found out that Cole and Allie had come to some kind of truce. Actually, she was pretty sure that Jess would be so thrilled that Allie no longer wanted to murder the man that Jess wouldn't say too much about it.

Before she could even get out of the car, Jess was at the door. "Are you all right? James told me that Cole said no one was hurt, but you sounded awful on the phone."

She slid out of the passenger seat and hugged her friend. "I'm fine, I promise. A little bruised ego perhaps, but that will heal. Cole's being really nice about the whole thing."

"I told you he was a good guy," Jess said. "Now maybe you'll give him a chance."

Cole came around the other side of the car. "None of that," he said. "We're starting fresh. I think we've both misunderstood a lot over the years, and we're going to put it behind us. However, I think it would be best if we did so without others jumping in and interfering. There's still a lot we need to work out, but I hope that in the end, we can find a way to be friends."

"Friends?" James said, coming around the corner. "I thought your sole goal in life was to marry Allie." He gave a teasing grin, and it made her feel sick. This was going to be the problem with becoming friends with Cole. People teased her mercilessly about his crush on her, and now that she no longer hated him, they'd tease her about that, too.

Cole caught her eye and shook his head. "Not anymore. I think both Allie and I have realized how different we are. We're not the same people we once were. I'd like to get to know the woman she's become, and I hope she'll give the guy I am a chance."

He looked so sincere, and for the first time, she wondered what his high school crush on her had cost him. She knew she'd been tormented mercilessly about him, but how much teasing had he gotten about her? Maybe she wasn't the only one who'd been humiliated. Maybe he'd been humiliated along with her. It seemed like all the things she thought were cut and dried were not so cut and dried after all.

Andrew's car pulled up, and she was grateful for the break from having to think about the situation. She'd called him on the way to Jess's house and asked him not to tell anyone what had happened. However, he'd brought along his fiancée, Layla. She should've expected her arrival, since they were basically inseparable these days. But she kind of hoped to have her brother to herself even if just for a few minutes. Plus, the fewer people who knew about her humiliation, the better. When Layla approached, Allie fought the urge to groan.

She knew that look. Although this was the first time

Allie had been on the receiving end of said look. Usually, Layla reserved that expression for when she was looking over Gram to make sure that Gram was all right, since Layla had been the nurse taking care of Gram when Gram had her health issues.

As Layla approached, she said, "I know Andrew said you said you're fine, but I want to make sure. And if I see any sign that you may not be fine, you're going to the doctor. People don't take their injuries from car accidents seriously."

Allie didn't bother hiding the groan that had been building, and Cole stepped away. Layla turned her head to look at him. "Don't you think you're going anywhere. You were in the accident too. You both need to be checked out."

Andrew grinned. "Good to see you again, Cole. I told you she was a feisty one. Don't argue with her and everything will turn out fine."

Layla made a noise, then directed Allie to go through a series of motions. She did as she was told, feeling sillier about the whole thing. And yet, part of her worried that one of them was hurt. She was glad that at least her brother and future sister-in-law had some sense of these matters. It wasn't like she had been in a lot of car accidents. This was her first one. She honestly didn't know what to do.

Once Layla was finished examining her, she said, "You should be all right. However, if you experience any pain, headaches, or just feel off, I want you to promise me that you'll see a doctor."

Allie nodded. "I will. I honestly didn't think this was a big deal."

"I know you didn't, and it may not be," Layla said. "But I'm just looking out for you, and I'd hate for you to be dealing with more serious injuries that could be a problem long-term."

As Layla turned to examine Cole, Allie looked at Jess. Her friend was looking sick again, and if this pregnancy was anything like her last, she probably wasn't feeling very well but, for the sake of everyone else, pretended to be just fine.

"And parched," Allie said. "Let's go inside and have a drink. I'm hoping you've got some of that famous lemonade of yours made." Most people hated Jess's lemonade, but Allie found a refreshing treat. Like Allie, Jess wasn't big on sweeteners. Jess nodded gratefully, like she'd been looking for an excuse to go inside and sit down.

When they got into the house, Jess immediately went to the fridge. "Give me a second, and I'll get it for you."

Allie shook her head. "That was just an excuse, and you know it. I can get my own lemonade. I want you to sit down and get your feet up. No offense, but you look exhausted."

Jess gave a bone-weary sigh. "Caitlin was up all night. Teething. I finally just got her down for a nap."

Allie poured them both a glass of lemonade. "Then why don't you go take a nap, and I'll make sure everyone gets some lemonade."

"I wouldn't want to be rude..." Not wanting to be rude or not, she looked ready to fall over. Ordinarily, she would be bustling around the kitchen, getting drinks for everyone, and fixing a plate of snacks, because that's what Jess did.

"I insist."

Jess looked toward the door. "I know you want to help, and I appreciate that. But I still haven't told James, and I don't want him suspicious. I don't want him to think anything is wrong. I don't usually take naps in the middle of the day."

Except when she was pregnant, Allie wanted to remind her, but that would probably only stress Jess out more. Especially if she hadn't yet told James. "Why the delay? You know he's going to be thrilled."

Jess picked up her glass of tea and took a long drink. "I know. I just want to find a special way of doing it, and I haven't come up with any great ideas."

Allie couldn't help smiling. Of course she wanted to make it special. That was one of the things that made Jess, Jess. She was always doing special things for others. Always trying to make others feel important. While most people would argue she should just tell James he was going to be a father again, Jess would make it a big event. So Allie could understand her hesitation. But her friend looked like she was about to fall over.

"At least go sit on the couch," Allie suggested, remembering the last time Jess had been pregnant, she fell asleep on almost any comfortable surface.

"That sounds like a great idea," Jess said. "Ignore the mess. We just brought out the Christmas decorations, but I haven't felt like doing anything with them. Cole's stuff is piled in there right now, at least until he decides what he's going to do. Both James and their family have all said that they'd love to see him stick around for a while. But he hasn't given anyone a definitive answer."

Then Jess gave her a pitying look. "I'm sorry, I understand you'd just as soon he leave. I just wish you could see him as we see the man we know him to be."

It was too soon in their detente for Allie to tell her that he might not be so bad after all. And frankly, she wasn't sure she wanted him to stay. That was an issue she had to sort out for herself, not discuss with her self-interested best friend.

Instead, Allie gave a lighthearted chuckle and said, "Weren't you the one who, on your wedding day, swore to hate Cole Anderson for the rest of his life because he canceled at the last minute for some Army mission?"

"Hey!" Jess said, sinking into the couch. "I told you I've forgiven him. We've worked through it and become friends. It took a lot of prayer and a lot of consideration. I'm so grateful for him now, but it didn't happen overnight."

Allie grinned at her friend. "So why are you expecting me to forgive him overnight?"

Jess's expression indicated that Allie's point had been made. For that, she was glad. She didn't fault her for forgiving her brother-in-law. But it was frustrating to have Jess continue to act like it should be this instantaneous thing. Even though their conversation by the side of the road had brought them to a much quicker understanding of one another than Allie would have thought.

"I understand what you're saying. You're right." Jess yawned as she leaned farther back into her couch. "We probably do try to make forgiveness more simplistic than it is. I should be more sensitive. Forgive me?"

Allie smiled as Jess pulled a blanket around herself. "You know I do. Just stop trying to throw us together, all right?"

"Mmm hmmm..." A soft snore escaped Jess's lips, and Allie was grateful that she was able to give her the chance to take a nap. Even more grateful that she wouldn't have Jess digging for info about the conversation between Allie and Cole while they waited for James. She wasn't sure she was ready to admit that she didn't hate him anymore.

But what was she supposed to feel, considering he had made high school miserable for her? True, more than ten years had passed, but the pain still felt fresh. Her discussion with Jess about forgiveness not being so easy weighed heavily on Allie's heart. There was that instantaneous decision of choosing to let go of a person's offenses, but it didn't change the pain of what had been done. Still, the conversation she'd just had with him had been pleasant. He'd been a lot nicer than she'd given him credit for.

Allie looked out the window to see Cole deep in conversation with her brother. Could she really avoid him for the next few weeks? And what if he stayed longer? Based on her conversation with him, he was a true friend to Andrew. Was it fair for her to hold on to her old wounds and make things uncomfortable for two people she loved?

Cole wasn't so bad. Surely, she could make peace with both him and all the people who liked to give her a hard time about things.

## 6

ole went to sit by Andrew as Layla packed up her things to put them in the car. James had invited them to stay for dinner, which Andrew had accepted. Cole just hoped that Allie wasn't too put out when she found out. His brother had gone inside to make the dinner plans with his wife.

He looked at Andrew. "Why didn't you tell me all those years ago that Allie didn't like me?"

Andrew gave him a funny look. "We did. We told you a lot. You never believed us."

He thought about his friend's words. Sure, the guys all told him that Allie hated his guts, but they had been laughing and smiling when they did.

"I thought you were kidding," Cole said. "You guys all acted like it was one big joke."

Andrew didn't say anything. He did look like he felt bad, though.

"Is that why you didn't tell me anything about Allie when I asked you the other day?" He let out a long sigh. "I feel like such a jerk, all those years, chasing after her, making a fool of myself. I just can't believe that you would let me do that."

Andrew gave him a guilty look. "I'm sorry. I guess back then, it was kind of fun to mess with my sister. I used to tease her about you all the time. It wasn't until we were adults, and I was going through some stuff, that we had a huge heart-to-heart about life and growing up together. I didn't know how much it had hurt her, to be honest. Allie is one of those people who doesn't often share her true feelings. Everyone thinks she does, because she's pretty outspoken about everything. But when it comes to her deep feelings, she lets very few people in."

Andrew frowned as he looked toward the house. "I know Allie took it in great stride," he said finally. "But all the times people teased her for being different, it really hurt her. Until she finally decided to be a rebel and completely not care."

Andrew turned thoughtful for a moment, then shook his head. "I don't know how much of this I should tell you. With all the interfering everyone else has done in our lives, Allie and I promised each other that we wouldn't do it to each other. I really don't want to interfere here. But I feel bad that you genuinely didn't know how hurt she was by everything. Anymore, I don't know what I was thinking at the time. But I can't tell you how much I regret not making you understand how she felt."

Cole thought about Andrew's words. There wasn't an easy answer. Growing up, he and his brother often fought over stupid things, and they were just as quick to give each other a hard time as they were to stand up for one another. Like cats and dogs, their aunt Helen used to say. Add in his cousins, and the ensuing sibling rivalry must have made their aunt and uncle want to tear their hair out. One never knew from one day to another if the cousins would be best friends or worst enemies.

Too bad this hadn't all been clearer back then. The truth was, even though he wanted to blame Andrew and their friends for not making it more obvious, he wasn't sure if he'd have listened. He'd been so far gone over Allie. Though he might have kept his feelings more to himself. And he probably would have done fewer humiliating activities. He'd like to think that he would have stopped had he realized just how much it hurt her.

"Thanks for talking this out with me," Cole said. "I'm not looking for you to be involved, or to interfere in any way. I want to respect Allie's wishes. I should have done so years ago."

The words felt good coming out, especially because he realized that's what he should have done in the first place. True, Allie used to run away when he came near, so he hadn't been able to talk to her to find out what her wishes were. But he should have taken the hint.

James came back outside, shaking his head. "Jess is asleep. I don't know what's wrong with her. She's been so tired lately. I know I said I'd help you with the car, but I'm starting to think I should do more to help Jess. Besides, I'm pretty sure if the insurance company had a look at the damage, they'd total it. It's going to take more to fix it than replace it."

Cole had suspected as much, but hearing it from his brother brought a heaviness to his heart. Allie was already worried about the cost of everything. How was she going to take this news?

"It'll be fine," Andrew said. "She has good insurance, so they'll cover the replacement. I don't think her deductible is too high."

Allie had mentioned paying the deductible would be a struggle. Add in the increase in premiums, and her financial situation looked bleak.

And it was partially his fault.

Cole looked toward the house. He couldn't see her accepting his help, not when she'd already fought him on this issue. But he had to do something.

"Can you find out what it is?" Cole said. "I'd like to cover it."

Andrew looked at him funny, like he thought he might have to go rounds with one of his oldest friends. "She hit you. I thought you'd just told me you were backing off on the crush thing. Money is not the way to my sister's heart."

But fighting with Andrew wasn't going to be necessary. He hoped. "And I was the one who just got her fired, making her so upset that she was distracted, driving on icy roads. I owe it to her to help somehow."

"Allie got fired?"

Andrew's question only made Cole feel worse. Hadn't she been telling him that she dreaded telling her family and hearing how disappointed they were in her?

"Yes, I did," Allie said, joining them. He hadn't noticed her approach. She turned and glared at him.

"This is why I told you to stay away from me. Why, did I ever think, even for a brief snatch of time, maybe, we could be friends? I was completely wrong. Maybe I do have a concussion or something after all. Because trusting you always gets me in trouble. I wanted to have some kind of plan in place before telling my family so that they could see I was taking responsibility for my life."

Shaking her head, Allie returned her attention to her brother and his fiancée. "Could you guys please keep this to yourselves? I know everyone's going to find out eventually, but I need time to get my head on straight."

Andrew gave his sister a hug, which is when she started crying. "We're here for you." He looked up at Layla, who nodded.

For a moment, he was jealous of his friend. The closeness he had with Allie, but also the way his fiancée looked so loving and supportive. Would he ever have that in his own life?

When Allie pulled away, Andrew looked up at him. "She'll take you up on your offer to cover her deductible. I didn't stand up for her enough when we were younger, and I should have been more forceful in letting you know just how unwelcome your attention was. But now, even though she doesn't want your money, I'm not letting her be too proud to accept it. I'll be in touch with the details. Please don't bother her with any of this."

Wow. That was the strongest hands-off message he'd ever gotten about her. But what else could he say but, "All right."

Andrew and Layla bundled Allie up into the car, and suddenly, she seemed far more fragile than she'd ever been.

It would have been easy to say that all of this was just a giant misunderstanding. Which it was. But Allie's current situation was Cole's fault. If only he understood why she'd hated him so much to begin with.

James patted him on the back. "It'll be all right. Andrew is really protective of Allie, and they've gotten to be close. Once this all dies down, it won't be so bad. Did you really get her fired?"

As they walked back into the house, Cole relayed the tale. When he got to the part about Jess sending him for the salve, James just shook his head.

"She's always had the crazy idea that if you two got married, she and Allie would be sisters. Allie is like a sister to her, so I hope that this doesn't ruin their friendship. Jess should have known better than to have sent you."

With a sigh, he shook his head. "When she was packing the baby up to go, I insisted on running the errand for her. I should have known something was up at how gleeful she got, but had I not volunteered, none of this would have happened."

It seemed like everywhere they ended up, it all led back to being his fault.

Each detail he gave to his brother only confirmed that belief.

The kitchen smelled wonderful as they entered. James patted Cole on the back again. "Don't let it get you down. Nadia has had it in for Allie for quite some time now. No one knows why. Allie has bent over backward, trying to befriend Nadia and get her approval. But everything she does only seems to make her angrier."

He knew all about that one. It was the story of his relationship with Allie. He did everything he could to show her how much he liked her and would be there for her, if only she let him. But it never seemed to work out that way.

The baby started crying in her bedroom, and James went to get her. The sound must have woken Jess up, because she entered the kitchen, yawning.

"Who started dinner? It smells wonderful."

It could only be one person. "Allie," he said.

Jess gave him a sleepy smile. "She's an amazing friend. I'm glad the two of you are willing to work through your differences so that hopefully you can find that out for yourself."

"I don't think that will be happening any time soon." It

shouldn't be so hard to admit his mistakes, but when he was crushing his sister-in-law's dream with those mistakes, it seemed almost impossible.

"Please tell me you didn't sing to her again."

The disgust in Jess's voice told him that he truly had been the only person to appreciate the trouble he'd gone to ask her to homecoming that year.

"No. I told her brother that I'd gotten her fired, and she saw that as a violation of her trust."

James entered the room, carrying the baby. "I've never seen her so upset. She seems really worried about how her family will react."

Based on the conversation he'd had with her earlier, he was inclined to agree. Jess's nod seemed to confirm it.

"You have to understand," Jess said. "Her parents have never agreed with how she lives. They think her lavender business is a stupid hobby, and that she should be doing more with her life. Which includes having a better job. I'm sure they will see the situation as a blessing in disguise, in terms of it being an opportunity for her to get a real job. That's not who she is. Personally, I see it as an opportunity for her to expand her lavender business. But her lack of capital is a real problem, and losing her employment means she has no more money to funnel into it."

Jess went to the stove and stirred whatever was in the pot. "Allie's problem is that she's too nice. People don't have the money to pay her, so she tells them to pay her when they can. She gives away a lot of her product because she doesn't want someone to do without something she believes will help them."

Then Jess looked over at Cole. "She started our dinner so I can rest, and cleaned up in here because that's the kind of person she is. Always looking for ways to help others, not thinking about herself."

"It sounds like she hasn't changed much since high school," Cole said. "That's why I've always liked her. I just want to help her because I know that no one else does. They're too busy taking from her."

Then he looked over at Jess. "Not you, of course. But your words remind me of how often she's overlooked because most people think that she won't mind."

"You have it worse than ever," James said. "Just don't go chasing after her this time."

They made him sound like a freak, or worse, a stalker. Was it wrong for him to notice her good points? Was it wrong for him to want to help her?

Apparently so. But after talking to both Allie and Andrew, Cole knew he would have to find a different way to be there for her. It was just a shame that someone who deserved good things in her life couldn't see that's all he wanted to do for her.

"I won't," Cole said. "I don't seem to know how to go about it the right way. I just don't understand, when all I ever did was try to be nice to her, how she could hate me so much."

Jess turned and looked at him with so much pity in her eyes that he wished he hadn't said anything. Then again, though it was hard hearing from Andrew that Allie legitimately hated him, at least it gave him enough sense to know that he needed to leave her alone. If he knew exactly what he'd done, he wouldn't do those things again, and hopefully, she'd realize he never meant her any harm.

"She doesn't like to be the center of attention, but all the stunts you pulled, thinking they were romantic, ended up putting her in a spotlight she didn't want. Worse, when people teased her about it, she felt humiliated."

Cole had always thought that people didn't notice Allie the way they should have or given her the credit she deserved. Until now, it hadn't occurred to him that maybe she didn't want it. Which was crazy, considering how he had gotten a great deal of unwanted attention when he'd been the youth worship leader in high school. He'd hated how people had put him on a pedestal and treated him like he was a rock star.

"I never realized," he said. "And that makes me feel terrible, because I know how that feels. It's why I gave up leading worship for the youth group."

James nodded. "I remember that. We all thought you were crazy. You were the best worship leader we'd had in youth group, and it seemed like you were being selfish in quitting."

"I was just tired of people making it about me, when I wanted it to be about the Lord."

Brother and sister-in-law both murmured sympathetically. It was nice they understood him so well, but it didn't solve the problem of what to do about Allie. The trouble with recognizing his similarities to her was that it only made him want to help her more. There was something about her that pulled at his heartstrings, and the fact he had played a role in her pain made him all the more determined to make it right for her.

The question was, how was he supposed to do that in a way that didn't make things worse? That wouldn't get him slapped with a restraining order?

Clearly, he'd made a lot of mistakes. Somehow, he had to find a way to make them right.

The baby fussed, and James sniffed her bottom. "Someone needs a change."

Which reminded Cole of the thing that had started today's nightmare. "I should get the salve out of my truck."

Even though it was frustrating Andrew and Allie had left so abruptly, missing out on what Cole had hoped would be a deepening of their friendship, when he saw how much snow had fallen, he was grateful they'd gotten back on the road when they had. The last thing he needed was another accident on his conscience.

When he passed Allie's car, he realized that one of the windows was open slightly.

Inside, everything was a terrible mess. How could she live like that? Worse, he didn't see her car keys, and snow was starting to drift into her vehicle. Knowing that it was going to be totaled, he wasn't so much worried about the interior getting damaged, but she seemed to have a lot of stuff that could get ruined.

Cole went to his truck, grabbed the salve and took it into the house. Then he grabbed one of the empty boxes from the laundry room. Of all the things he'd ruined for her, he could at least keep the stuff she kept in her car safe. He didn't want to be blamed for messing up something else of hers.

He made quick work of piling her belongings into the box. And even though he tried very hard not to pry by looking through them, he couldn't help noticing how many of the papers had the bright red markings indicating the bill was past due.

How had she let everything get so bad in her life?

None of his business. He continued putting her things in the box. He'd have Jess run it to her in the morning. That way, he could keep his promise to Andrew and Allie that he would leave Allie alone.

But he couldn't stop thinking about those bills.

How was she going to pay them if she didn't have a job?

Jess had said that a lot of people owed her money, but Allie was too nice to collect. Somehow, he couldn't see her going after them, even though she was in dire straits.

Was there a way he could help her financially, without her feeling like she was taking a handout? Andrew had been so forceful in telling him- and her- that she would accept Cole's help with the deductible, that he suspected she would not have said yes otherwise.

These bills seemed to be numerous enough that whatever severance check Allie would get probably wouldn't cover them.

Cole brought the box into the house. Jess was dishing up dinner and James held a much happier looking Caitlin.

"Snow was blowing into Allie's car, and I didn't want her things to be ruined. Can you take this to her?"

Jess nodded. "Of course. I know it sounded like we were being hard on you earlier, and I'm sorry if we were too harsh. I really do think if Allie would give you a chance, you guys would be good together. But until today, I don't think I realized just how much pain Allie continues to carry. Honestly, what I regret the most is my role in all this. I should never have tried to force you two together."

He knew she was trying to make him feel better, but her words only made him feel more conflicted. If others thought that Allie and Cole would be so good together, then why did Allie fight it so hard? And why did things end so badly between them?

However, Jess did have a point. Every time he was around Allie, Cole felt pressure to try to force things. To make her see that he wasn't so bad, and that he truly cared for her. Maybe it was time to let Allie go.

*Lord, I don't know if Allie and I are meant to be. But I do know that as much as I try to make her like me, it always backfires. You know my heart, and you know Allie's. Bring us together in a way that lets us know that it's Your will. If it's not Your will, please help me love and respect her from an appropriate distance.*

Sometimes when he prayed, he felt an immediate sense of relief. Though that wasn't the case today, he had to trust that by giving it to God, he was doing the right thing. And in that, was comfort.

He hoped that, in time, whatever God's answer was about Allie, he would feel confident in it. Because right now, everything inside him was a mass of doubt and wondering about how best to handle the situation.

# 7

When Allie returned home, she went straight to her greenhouse. There, she could be among her lavender plants and find comfort. Everything had gone wrong today, and though she could almost hear Jess's voice in the back of her head, telling her to look for the blessing in disguise, all she could do was wonder how any of this was going to be okay.

Footsteps sounded behind her, and she turned to see Gram entering the greenhouse.

"Rough day?" Gram asked, holding out a cup of tea.

She nodded. She knew Andrew hadn't ratted her out, but Gram had always known here better than anyone else. Something Allie had said or done had tipped her off that things weren't right.

"So bad, I don't even know where to begin."

As she sipped the tea, she could feel Gram's eyes on her. Most people thought Gram was a pushy old lady, but she always seemed to know that with Allie, she shouldn't push.

"Does it have anything to do with the return of Cole Anderson?"

"So, Andrew did tell you."

Gram shook her head. "No, but I was at the church earlier, and the pastor mentioned to me that his nephew has been home since last week. I don't know why, but it just seems like things go wrong for you whenever he's around."

Finally. Someone who understood and didn't think she was crazy. She launched into the whole story, and Gram nodded and murmured in all the appropriate places. For the first time since Cole had been in the store, she felt safe. Like somehow this whole nightmare would turn out all right.

When she was finished, however, Gram looked at her the way she always did when she was about to deliver bad news.

"Do you ever wonder why some people keep turning up like a bad penny?"

She shook her head.

"I always figured it was because God had something to teach us. If there's someone I can't stand, He always manages to keep putting that person in my path until I figure out a way to see him or her through God's eyes, and love them anyway. For example, did you know that my good friend Mona used to be my enemy?"

Allie tried not to choke on her tea. "You two are thick as thieves. And while I don't think you guys would ever literally steal something, we all live in fear of the day we're going to have to bail you out of jail for one of your crazy stunts."

"Save your money." Gram gave a wicked grin. "There's a part of me that always wondered what happens on the inside. I've just never been brave enough to do something wrong enough to land me there."

It figured. At least Allie knew that there was something in this world that Enid Bigby was afraid of.

"So why were you and Mona enemies?"

She crossed her arms over her chest. "Because she stole my boyfriend. And then, she stole the job I applied for from right under my nose. It seemed like everything I wanted in life, Mona always took it. No matter how hard I tried, Mona was always better. Do you know, she even stole the name I wanted for my firstborn daughter? Since I was a little girl, I was going to have a daughter named Brenda. But what happened when she had her daughter before I did? She named her Brenda. So of course, I couldn't have a daughter named Brenda. Because everyone would think I was copying Mona."

Keeping a straight face during her rant was more difficult with each transgression listed.

"So how did you stop hating Mona?"

A tender look crossed her face. "We were in Bible study together, and we had to draw the name of a person in the group to pray for every day. And of course, I got Mona. At first, I was mad at God, because how dare He make me be nice to someone so horrible? Then, I started reading in Job, listening to God's questions about man daring to know God's heart. And I realized, who was I to hate Mona, a woman God loved? So, I began to pray for her and do nice things for her, and I prayed for myself, asking God to give me His heart for Mona."

Tears filled Gram's eyes, and Allie took her hand. For some reason, she noticed how much older Gram's hand seemed to be. Worn. Like it was filled with the wisdom of all those years of living.

"I failed to mention that in all my hating of Mona, she hated me just as much. I know not a lot of people have liked me over the years, thinking I was too opinionated, too strong-willed, and all that. Mona especially hated those things about me. But as I prayed, I felt compassion for her. I realized that the boyfriend she stole from me, well, she married him and he turned out to be a terrible man. The job I wanted ended up being a horrible job that made her miserable. And Brenda? She fell in with a bad crowd after having an affair with a married man. Her life went into an awful downward spiral. Everything I envied about Mona was a curse to her. And she hated how my life seemed to be so wonderful because all she saw was the outside. It wasn't until I started praying for her that I realized all these things."

Allie squeezed her hand. Even if Gram had not said that her heart had changed, Allie could see it. Though it pained her to admit, she could even see how the story applied to her. In all the years she had hated Cole Anderson, she'd not once prayed good things about him. Mostly it had been, "God, please don't let me see him today," and then she'd get mad at God because he would invariably cross her path.

"It took several years for Mona and me to become friends, and while I never prayed to be her friend, even after our Bible study was over, I committed to praying for her every single day. When she and I finally had a heart-to-heart after all those years, we realized all the things we had in common. We realized how silly we'd been for holding the different things against one another."

The tender look Gram gave her made Allie feel loved. "I think about all the different people in my life, and I've come to realize that God gives me the most difficult ones to teach me something. I don't know what He wants you to learn from Cole, but I think it's time that you stop running from whatever it is, and ask God to help you see whatever He wants you to see. Otherwise, Cole is going to keep turning up, and it's going to keep messing with you."

Allie couldn't imagine anything worse than her current

situation. But every time she thought the Cole problem couldn't get worse, it always found a way to do so.

What harm could it do to pray for Cole?

"How long did you have to pray for Mona before it started to work?" Allie asked.

Gram let out a sigh. "Too long. Mostly because of my own stubborn pride. What I didn't tell you about Brenda is that she died. Right about the same time my son Adam did. I saw Mona in church, and I realized that she was the only person in that entire place who understood what I was going through. And I was the only person who could understand her pain. How could I hate someone when it was clear we both needed each other?"

Allie couldn't ever imagine needing Cole. His brand of help almost always made things worse for her. But she supposed that Gram never would have imagined the circumstances that would help her realize she needed Mona.

"He is going to cover my deductible," Allie said. "I wouldn't call that needing each other, but I will admit that, as much as it pains me to take his money, it is a weight off my shoulders."

Gram gave her a sympathetic look. "I wish I could do more to help you. But I know that if I give you any money, those bloodsucking vulture children of mine would say that you've done something to abuse me into forcing my actions. Everything was so much easier when Adam was alive."

This was the second time Gram had mentioned her deceased son in this conversation. Uncle Adam was one of the topics that had always been off-limits in the Bigby household. Allie's problems seemed so minor in comparison to the pain of losing her son that her grandmother carried with her every day.

"You're talking about him a lot more," Allie said. "Has something new happened, or is there something going on I should know about?"

She shook her head. "No, but the more I see my children attacking me, attacking you guys, and trying to take over the farm, I keep wondering why. What did I do wrong to make my children value money over family? We all used to be so close, and I don't understand how we've all grown apart."

The sadness in her voice made Allie's heart hurt. She'd heard her parents' rants over the years, and seen the tension in her cousin Caroline's family. True, Gram could be highly critical of others and a bit annoying at times, but deep down, she always had a good heart. Allie had never had a problem with her, mostly because she liked the fact that Gram always said exactly what she thought. There was no guessing, no trying to decipher the hidden meaning. It was what it was. And that was a rare thing in the world today.

Then Gram let out a long sigh. "I wish I'd stayed in better touch with Adam's wife and daughter. I don't know if you remember Madison or not, but she was the cutest little girl, full of life and sunshine. I lost touch with them years ago, and I know it was partially because Shannon thought I was too bossy."

Tears filled her eyes again as she looked over at Allie. "I know I haven't always been a good person and a lot of people don't like me. But I always meant well. I thought with my criticism, that I was giving suggestions for improvement people would want to take and use to better themselves. I couldn't understand why anyone wouldn't want to be better. However, as I look back, I wish I could've had your generous spirit towards others."

Allie had no idea what to say in response. She had her own lack of generosity, her own flaws. But that wasn't what worried her the most. Why was Gram being so melancholy and looking back at things she couldn't change?

"You're not sick, are you?" Allie studied her grandmother's face, looking for any sign that she wasn't giving a truthful answer.

An innocent expression stared back at her. "No. My health is under control now. But we're only given today to live our lives, so we have to do the best we can with each moment we have. When I look back at all my regrets and I hear how you're struggling, the only thing I can do is share my heart, and let you know the mistakes I made so you don't do the same. I know the situation with Cole is difficult, but if you let your dislike of him continue to consume you, it will ruin your life. God is big enough that He will take care of Cole if you're willing to let go of everything you hold against him."

"Thanks. You're right. I know I haven't been praying for him the way I should. And I have been rather stingy with the grace when it comes to Cole."

There was no judgment in Gram's expression, only love. "If you want to move things along faster, I have a wonderful cabbage cleanse that will do you a world of good. It will help release all of your negative energy that's holding you back."

And that was the Enid everyone knew and loved to hate. As far as Allie knew, none of Gram's cleanses had any backing in scientific evidence. And mostly, rather than curing anyone of anything, all they did was give people a stomach ache.

"I'll pass, thanks."

"You don't know what you're missing," Gram said, looking slightly disappointed. "But you know, now that I think about it, the rest of the family could benefit. Especially that father of yours. Now he's trying to get me to have one of those voice-activated computer thingies in the house. What do I need with some computer listening in on everything I say? It's probably just a way for people to spy on me."

Allie had been trying to stay out of this fight between her grandmother and her parents. Actually, she tried to stay out of all the fights, because she didn't want to get involved. No matter what she did, someone would consider her actions a betrayal, and it always felt like no matter what she did, she couldn't win.

As she tried to think of an answer to Gram's waiting expression, the barn door opened and Wade Ellis, one of their neighbors, entered. Wade had bought the farm next door a couple of years back. At the time, Allie had been frustrated because she'd been eyeing that piece of property herself to grow more lavender. But, Allie hadn't had the money, and the bank hadn't been willing to take a risk on her. Given that her lavender business still hadn't really taken off, the bank had probably been right. And Wade had become a good friend to them. He'd liked her brother Andrew's tiny house so much that he had built one of his own. Now that her cousin Caroline and her fiancé Hayden had put several tiny houses on Bigby Farm as guest rentals, they'd hired Wade as a handyman to help them keep up with all the work.

"Allie! Andrew told me I could find you in here. I wanted to give my mother a nice gift for Christmas. I know she doesn't recognize me anymore, and the gesture will be lost on her, but I thought perhaps you had some kind of cream or other lavender product that would make her feel more comfortable. I'd also like to give the nurses in the Alzheimer's unit at Retro Village something nice to express my appreciation for the good care they're giving her."

Allie thought for a moment. Though she made several

quality anti-aging creams, Mrs. Ellis wasn't worried about wrinkles at this phase in her life. The nurses were much easier. Many of them bought products from her at the Farmer's Market, so they would be easy to choose the right product for.

"Why don't I come with you the next time you visit your mother, and I can see what would be best for her. That way, I can also scope out the nurses to see which ones have purchased products from me before and I can give them something they really like."

Wade gave her a big grin. "Allie, you're a gem. That's going above and beyond. Thank you. Be sure to add on a little something extra to your bill for your trouble."

Allie shook her head. "There is no extra. You're a friend, and that's what friends do for each other."

"Not when that friend just got fired from her job," Gram said, glaring at Allie. "You graciously accept whatever extra people want to pay you, and you tell them thank you."

Wade stared at her. "They fired you from the Gas N' Shop? What were they thinking, getting rid of the only decent employee they had there?"

Though it was nice to have Wade's support, Allie also didn't feel like constantly rehashing the situation. Which was why she really wasn't looking forward to everyone knowing. Each time, she was going to have to explain things, and she didn't want to hear everyone's pity, or worse, having the old teasing about Cole come back.

"It's a long story," Allie said. "I'd rather not get into it, if you don't mind. It's going to be bad enough having to face my parents as soon as I get back to the house."

Wade made a sympathetic noise. "Andrew told me they were staying here through the wedding. I don't know why they couldn't just get a room at the B&B. It sounds like they're making everyone crazy."

Crazy didn't even begin to describe it. Though all of the Bigby cousins tried really hard not to make the family drama public, someone like Wade, who was at the farm almost daily, couldn't help getting a taste of it.

"It's almost enough to make me move out," Allie said. "But as Gram so helpfully reminded me, I'm now out of a job."

"You could come stay at my farmhouse. Now that I'm living in a tiny house like I've always dreamed, the place is just sitting empty. I haven't been able to figure out what I want to do with it. I'd like the place to be used for a good cause, but there aren't any charities who can use a falling-down farmhouse in the middle of the country. It would be nice to have someone living there, just keeping an eye on things. I'm always afraid the pipes will freeze or something like that, and I won't notice until it's too late."

So now Allie she was a charity case. This was one more reason on top of all of the others that she didn't want people knowing about her job situation.

"It sounds an awful lot like-"

"A fantastic opportunity for Allie," Gram said, giving her a stern look. "Playing referee between her parents and her is driving me crazy. And, because her mother, Mary, is so particular about things, Allie has had to move most of her product making into the barn. That's what her little work-shop off her greenhouse was supposed to be, but I've noticed that it's too full of plants for her to work. The barn isn't heated, just the greenhouse, and I've been worried about her working out there in the cold. A whole house to herself will give her space to catch up on all of her product orders."

Even if she had wanted to argue with her grandmother, she wouldn't have been able to. Not only was Gram correct in her assessment of the situation, but she was impressed with how much Gram seemed to notice about what was going on with her lavender business. That was one of the reasons why, even though Jess saw this as an opportunity for her to expand her lavender business, she had known such thoughts were futile. Everything in the house was wedding central, and there was simply no space for her to do her work.

"That settles it then," Wade said with a smile. "You probably have too much stuff to put in your car, and I know it will take several trips, but if you point me to the things that you need here in the barn, I'm happy to put them in my truck and bring them over."

Then she sighed. As good as it sounded to be able to go and have her own place, her own space, even if just for little while, without a car, it was impossible. Though Wade's farm was just next door, the idea of next-door was a bit of a misnomer, considering his house was a mile away as the crow flies, longer by car.

"I was just in a car accident," Allie said. "I don't have transportation."

Could she sound any more pathetic? At least Allie wasn't trying to impress Wade for any reason. They'd gone out on one date after he first moved to Arcadia Valley, and they had mutually agreed afterward that there would never be anything between them other than friendship. The spark just hadn't been there. But, at least it had given her the chance to become friends with Wade, and to let go of any residual anger she might have had about him buying the farm she'd wanted for herself. How funny that she would now be living there.

Wade looked at her like he was about to have another difficult conversation with her. "I know I've already probably reached my limit of how far I can push your pride, but it would be foolish of me not to tell you that you are free to use one of my cars until you figure out what to do about yours. I usually drive my truck around. My mom's old car is just sitting in the garage. I take it out from time to time to keep everything running smoothly, but mostly it just sits. Again, you would be doing me a favor by driving it."

What did they say about beggars not being able to be choosers? That didn't fully apply here, except that given her circumstances, she couldn't say no to the use of a car. Not when everyone else here needed their cars, and it would be selfish of her to expect them to drive her places or let her borrow their car when they had their own things to do.

"I guess I can't say no," Allie said. "But you have to let me know if I'm being a burden or an inconvenience in any way. And once I get back on my feet, I will insist on paying rent."

The good thing about being friends with Wade, was that he knew better than to argue. He nodded slowly. "When the time comes, we can work something out."

They made arrangements, and Allie went to the house to pack a bag. She wouldn't take all of her stuff right then, since she didn't know how long the arrangement would last, but she would have at least a few things to get her by for several days. When she entered her room, any doubts about staying in Wade's old house disappeared. Her bed was covered with a bunch of baskets that would be filled with flowers for centerpieces at the wedding reception. Once again, her mother had taken over her room and invaded her space without her permission.

She went to her closet and began pulling out items of clothing. Even her closet hadn't been considered sacred, because her clothes had been shoved to one side, and table linens on hangers were on the other. Her mother always waited until she went to work to do this sort of thing, and when she got home, Gram would always apologetically tell her that she had done her best.

No wonder Gram had been so eager for her to accept Wade's offer.

She pulled a duffel bag from under her bed, and filled it with the clothes she had taken from her closet. How strange that she could become an adult and not own a suitcase. But, as she grabbed the duffel bag, she was grateful she had at least these. They'd been useful in helping her haul her lavender products to the farmers market. Then, she took what she needed out of her drawers and looked around her room for anything else she might need. Because of all the changes at the house over the past year, Allie had done a good job paring down excess belongings and getting rid of things she didn't need. A lot of her most treasured items were in boxes from when Hayden had come to stay with them as part of Gram's challenge to get people to understand that farm life was still a good life. Hayden had been given Allie's room, and Allie had moved upstairs to one of the tiny attic rooms that had been her cousin Caroline's. Until that point, Caroline had had the whole upstairs to herself, which seemed like a lot of space, until a person considered how small the space really was. In parts of the rooms, the ceiling was so low that a person couldn't even stand up all the way.

Allie had finally been able to move back into her own room when wedding madness had descended upon them a few months ago. So maybe it wasn't terrible that she hadn't been able to unpack yet. She could do so at Wade's house. Although, was it right to fully move in? Is that what Wade had intended when he offered her the place, or was it simply a temporary respite from the insanity at Bigby Farm?

She sighed as she grabbed her two duffel bags. This would be enough to get started, along with the items she told Wade to bring from the barn. As she entered the living room, she ran into her mother.

"Allison! Where are you going? The wedding is in two weeks. We need you here to help us get ready. You can't go on a trip."

Once again, she tried hard not to cringe at the use of her full name. No matter how many times she explained that she preferred to be called Allie, her mother insisted she had named her Allison for a reason, and declared it a personal insult that Allie had chosen to go by a nickname. Such was the nature of her war with her mother.

"I'm not going on a trip. Wade knows space is tight here, and he thought perhaps I would be more comfortable staying at his house. Considering my bed is currently covered with baskets, that sounds like a good idea. This will give you guys more room for wedding preparations, and I won't worry about where to sleep."

Her mother made the same noise she always made when she was disgusted. "I don't know why you just can't be happy for your brother. After all he's been through, and the loss he suffered, it wouldn't kill you to get on board with his wedding."

One more symptom of the problem. No matter what Allie said, her mother always had to give it her own inter-pretation, one that had no bearing in reality.

"I am happy for Andrew. And I love Layla. I can't imagine two people more perfect for one another. That's not what this is about. I just need my own space, and Wade has kindly offered it to me."

Her mother's face twisted in disgust. "Wade? You don't mean the homeless guy your cousin hired out of pity, do you?"

This was why they could never have a conversation. Everyone knew that Wade owned the farm next door. They knew that the farm had a house. They all also knew that, for whatever reason, Wade preferred to live in a tiny house he'd built himself.

"Wade is not homeless. Just because he has a thick beard and wears old clothes all the time doesn't make him homeless. He does a lot of messy work, so he can't exactly wear a three-piece suit every day."

"Are you mocking me?" Her mother asked, snarling.

All right, so technically she had been a little snarky in her response. But this was what being around her mother did to her. As she opened her mouth to give another retort, she remembered what Gram had said in the barn.

Part of why Gram was eager for her to stay at Wade's was the tension between Allie and her mother. It was easy to blame her mother for all of their problems. But she knew she wasn't doing the relationship any favor with her attitude.

"I'm sorry," she said. "I've had a rough day, and I should have been kinder in my answer."

Her mother sniffed the way she did when Allie's best answer was still not good enough. Because nothing she did was ever good enough.

"I didn't even know you were here," her mother said. "Your car isn't in the driveway."

At least if she told her mother now, she could make her escape and avoid the lecture. Plus, since her dad wasn't here, she wouldn't have them going at her with both barrels.

"I was in a car accident on my way home from work. My car is likely totaled, so Andrew and Layla came to get me."

"How could you be so selfish? Their wedding is two weeks away, and you take them away from wedding preparations? You might say that you're not jealous, but it's just like you to add drama and pull them in to distract them. I think you're subconsciously trying to sabotage the celebration."

A normal mother would have asked her if she was okay. Or she would've said something like, "I'm glad you're not hurt." Even Gram, who was not known to be the world's most sensitive human being, had offered comfort as her initial response to Allie's situation.

"Believe what you want. Nothing I say or do seems to make it any different. Wade is waiting, so I'll see you when I see you."

She tried to walk away, but her mother grabbed one of the duffel bags.

"So that's what this is. You're jealous of your brother's wedding, so you're running off to live in sin with a homeless man."

If Andrew had been present, he and Allie would have laughed about how ridiculous that statement was. How was it even possible to live in sin with a homeless man? That would imply having a place to live, which would make the man not homeless. Also, her mother rejected Christianity as being too simplistic for educated people. Which meant her mother had no concept of the idea of living in sin.

Allie just shook her head. "Once again, you're drawing the wrong conclusion. I'd explain it to you, but you wouldn't understand."

This time, when she turned away, her mother let her. As she walked out the door with her bags, Wade rushed over to help her. It had stopped snowing, and leaving only a couple of inches on the ground. But there was something in the air that told her it was going to be a long, hard winter, even if it was only in her heart.

Gram had encouraged her to pray for Cole and to find a way to love him, but as Wade drove away, she wondered if she should find a different way to pray for her parents as well.

## 8

A week after the accident, Cole still felt at a loss in trying to figure out his purpose for the future. Allie still hated him, or so he assumed. Andrew was supposed to stop by Arcadia Valley Community Church later today to pick up a check for Allie. Since returning home, he had been helping Uncle Vince, the pastor, with things around the church. Odd jobs that needed to get done, and it felt good to be useful. He'd never been the sort to sit around and watch TV while on vacation. And that's all this could be. While part of him had secretly hoped that his time here would give him a reason to stay, he wasn't sure living in the same town as Allie was a good idea.

When he walked into Uncle Vince's office, all thoughts of her were banished as he noticed the look on his uncle's face.

"What's wrong?"

He was almost afraid to ask, the man's expression was so somber.

"That was Jerry, Agnes Day's husband. She's just back from the doctor, and her condition is more serious than they thought. They're traveling to California later in the week to see a specialist. Agnes is upset that she won't be leading worship on Sunday, but I'm more worried about how she's going to be."

Of course, Uncle Vince would be more worried about Agnes than about the Sunday service. Anyone could lead worship, but Agnes was special.

"I'm so sorry. You think she'll be all right?"

Uncle Vince shook his head. "I don't know. Jerry didn't give me very many details, and Agnes was crying too hard for me to understand."

Agnes Day never cried. She was known for making everyone else cry with her beautiful music. True, some people thought her conviction that worship music still had to be played on the church's ancient organ was old-fashioned. But there was something beautiful about the way she made those hymns come alive. It had been why Cole had fallen in love with worship music. Especially when she'd started giving him music lessons when he'd been a teenager.

Agnes might've been a stickler for church music on the organ, but she'd encouraged Cole to play a variety of instruments. Even now, just the thought of it warmed his heart and made him feel safe.

"I know you said you would never lead worship again," Uncle Vince said. "But the church needs you. Agnes needs you. Would you be willing to fill in for her until she returns? Otherwise, we might have to cancel the Christmas program."

His uncle could have asked him to do anything and he would have gladly agreed. Anything but this. But even as his lips moved to form the word, "No," his vocal chords weren't so cooperative.

"Yes," he said.

Maybe saying stupid things wasn't just limited to his experience with Allie. After all, agreeing to lead worship, even temporarily, was about the stupidest thing he had ever said.

His uncle beamed, and some of the weight appeared to come off his shoulders. Though Uncle Vince still seemed sad, he no longer appeared to be worried.

"No one else can do it?" Cole asked.

Uncle Vince shook his head. "None who would for the right reasons," he said.

If he hadn't already agreed to do it, those words would've changed his mind. While he certainly had no knowledge of what a rock star's experience might be like, when he'd led youth group worship back in high school, he'd known that being the rock star of Arcadia Valley Community Church was more pressure than he could handle. He'd stepped down near the middle of his senior year, having already enlisted in the Army, citing that as the reason for them needing to replace him. But in truth, he was glad for the excuse because it had never sat well with him to be elevated to godlike status.

Why no one ever treated Agnes like a god, he didn't know. Maybe it was because when they were in high school, they all thought Agnes must be nearing one hundred years old. Of course, back then anyone over thirty was thought to be at death's door. But here he was, at that age, a little wiser about the number of years a person had to live, and suddenly the weight of Agnes's condition fell upon him.

"Just how old is she, anyway?" Cole asked, looking at his uncle.

"Her kids had a big party for her 85th birthday last year. Some people might that think that's pretty old, but just last week, she and the Grannies were out taking turns racing on four-wheelers."

Cole stared at his uncle. *What on earth?* "Who are the Grannies, and what were they thinking, putting an old lady in a four-wheeler race?"

Uncle Vince laughed. "That's right, I'd forgotten. A few years ago, Mona Henderson's husband died. I don't know if you remember Earl or not, but he was a controlling man, and when she found herself a widow, she decided to do all the things she'd never been allowed to do before. She and several elderly women in our community already had a knitting group that also did other projects, so they turned it into a club they called the Grannies. And let me tell you, those old ladies are wilder than any group of teenagers I've ever known."

"And Agnes is part of them?"

His uncle grinned. "As a matter of fact, she is. More alive and full of life than she was even back when you knew her. Which is why I can't believe this news. I know everyone has to die sometime, but I just can't imagine what this church is going to be like without Agnes."

The somber look returned to his uncle's face.

"This worship leader thing isn't going to be temporary, is it?" Cole asked, hating that he already knew the answer, but that he felt compelled to ask anyway.

"Agnes has been talking about retiring for years. We've never liked any of the candidates who applied for the position when we posted it. Every time we would be close to hiring someone, Agnes would come to church and tell me she didn't have peace in her heart about us making that decision. And I'll admit, I felt the same lack of peace. Maybe having you here-"

"Don't even say it." Cole had known his uncle long

enough to know the words that would come next. "I won't have any circumstances in which Agnes is ill be considered a blessing."

Uncle Vince shook his head. "We have to see both the good and the bad from the Lord as a blessing. But you have to admit that having you home at the time we needed you most is a blessing indeed."

"But I'm not here forever. It's just a break. Just until I figure out what I'm to do with my life now that the Army doesn't want me."

Uncle Vince gave him the same sad look he always gave him when he talked about his discharge. True, it was an honorable discharge. After being injured in a jump gone wrong, Cole's back would never be the same. The doctors had said he was unfit to continue performing his duty.

The only dream Cole Anderson had for his life had been taken from him, and there was nothing he could do about it. So why on earth would his destiny be to come home to the very thing he'd run away from?

As if he needed the reminder of all his broken dreams, Andrew knocked on the office door. "Pastor Harris?"

"Andrew, come in. Cole and I were just talking about some bad news I received. I understand Agnes was supposed to play for your wedding next week here in the church."

The smile on Andrew's face told Cole everything he needed to know about the impending wedding. Though Andrew had already given Cole a very happy retelling of his romance with Layla when they'd met at El Corazon, it still made Cole feel good to see how the thought of marriage brought so much joy to his friend. But then Andrew frowned.

"What bad news? Everything is all right, isn't it?"

"Agnes's illness is worse than she initially thought. She'll be in California during your wedding."

Andrew looked like he was processing the pastor's words. "But the Christmas pageant is the next day. Who will you get to take over on such short notice? I'm sure we can find CDs or something to play at the wedding, but it would be a shame to miss out on an important Christmas tradition in Arcadia Valley. It's why we delayed our honeymoon."

Funny how Andrew was more worried about the Christmas pageant that served their community than he was about his own wedding. That was what Cole had always liked about the Bigby siblings. Their concern was always for others, not themselves.

Uncle Vince smiled at Andrew. "Cole has agreed to lead worship in Agnes's absence. He has also agreed to take over the Christmas pageant."

The look Andrew gave him made Cole feel like perhaps their friendship wasn't over after all. "That's great news. I know you were never comfortable on stage, but I still miss the times when you led worship for youth group. I wouldn't want to impose, but if you'd be willing to take Agnes's place at our wedding as well, it would mean a lot to us. I know I said I could get CDs, but I know it would be a disappointment to Layla."

Cole remembered how much it had hurt Jess when, at the last minute, he hadn't been able to come to his brother's wedding. But his team had been chosen for an emergency mission, and Cole had had no choice but to go. Jess eventually forgave him, and even though this wasn't the same situation, it felt almost like he would be making up for his mistake by preventing another wedding disaster.

But then there was Allie.

"I would gladly perform for your wedding. In fact, I

would consider it a great honor. But I also know Allie's feelings toward me, and the last thing I want is to ruin your special day because of how badly I've hurt your sister."

Andrew nodded slowly, like he hadn't thought about that part. "That does present a problem. Until now, I'd even forgotten that I was mad at you for getting her fired."

Then Andrew chuckled. "But you've always been a good friend to me, and now that I've had a week to think about what happened, I know I was too hard on you. I said a lot of things to you in anger, and it was wrong. I'm very sorry for how I treated you. It's humbling to know that even after that, you'd still be willing to play at my wedding."

At least Cole had been right in that his friendship would be able to get beyond the troubles with Allie. But it didn't mean he was willing to add fuel to the fire.

"Of course, I forgive you. I'm truly sorry for everything I've done to hurt Allie. I don't want any of this to come between us."

Then Cole turned to Uncle Vince. "You've been like a father to me all these years. And I don't know if this is fatherly advice or pastoral advice, but I sure could use some help in figuring out what to do. I want to honor Allie's feelings, but I also want to be there for my friend. Is there a way to do both?"

"I can see where having you play at Andrew's wedding would upset her," Uncle Vince said.

Before Uncle Vince could continue, Layla and Mary, Andrew's mother entered the office, flanked by Andrew's grandmother.

"What's this about Allison causing more drama?" Mary asked, her face scrunched up like a volcano about to burst.

Andrew sighed. "There is no drama. Allie hasn't caused anything."

"But he just said that if he plays at your wedding, Allison will be upset." Cole had heard that Allie's mother had always been hard on her, but this was the first he'd seen of it. She didn't even know the full story, and she was already casting stones at Allie.

Uncle Vince stood. Then he turned his attention to Layla. "I was just telling Andrew the unfortunate news that Agnes is ill and will be unable to play for your wedding. We were just discussing alternative options for music."

Layla went over to Andrew and put her arm around him. "That's terrible. Agnes is such a sweetheart. Is there anything we can do?"

Mary made a noise. "That old bag is still alive and kicking? It's terrible, of course, that you don't have someone to do your wedding music, but there are worse tragedies. Having to listen to the noise coming from that organ is one of them."

With a glare that one didn't often see from the ordinarily patient man, Uncle Vince said, "Mary, that's enough. I realize they do things differently in Seattle, but in this church, we don't speak like that of others. Agnes is a much-beloved member of our community, and we will be praying for her recovery. The question is, at least as it relates to everyone in this room, is what to do about the wedding music."

Then Uncle Vince turned to Layla. "Thank you for your concern for Agnes. We don't know all the details yet, but as soon as I have something I can pass on, I'll let everyone know."

At Layla's nod, Cole found he had a greater respect for his old friend and his friend's bride. Most women would be upset that a little over a week before her wedding, the plan was drastically changing.

Layla looked up at Andrew. "I don't really care about the music, as long as we're married."

"I feel the same way," Andrew said, bending down and giving her a quick kiss.

"We have to have good music," Mary said, looking indignant. "This is an important occasion, one that people will remember for years."

He felt sorry for Allie and Andrew having such a mother. None of her words displayed any concern for her children as people. Just for her agenda.

"I think what people will remember is how much Layla and Andrew love each other," Cole said, smiling at his friend. "I hope someday I find a love like yours."

Andrew smiled back. "I pray you will, too. Even if it's not with my sister."

Years before, that comment would have stung. But now, he saw it for what it was. His friend supported him, and wished him happiness wherever it took him. Even if it meant giving up on Allie. There was a lightness in his heart at the thought. All these years, he'd wanted her. And still, he did want someone with the kindness, generosity and free spirit that Allie had. But he wanted someone to love him the way Layla loved Andrew.

"It no longer has to be," Cole said.

Enid, Andrew's grandmother, cleared her throat. Cole had forgotten she was even there. "So now, let's talk music. I believe we just walked in on a conversation where Andrew and Cole were debating about whether or not Cole should play at Andrew's wedding, given the history between Cole and Allie."

"I didn't know you were musical," Layla said, turning her attention to him. "It must be wonderful to have so much talent."

"He will be filling in for Agnes during our worship services." Uncle Vince's voice was filled with pride, and he was glad he had said yes to helping out.

Mary made a noise. "I suppose we could audition him."

The woman had a knack for making everything about her. And once again, he was sad to think that was the kind of mother Allie had. Though his mother had died when he was young, what he remembered most was how he'd felt so loved by her. And even when Aunt Helen took over, he never doubted that his family loved him.

"I don't have time for auditions," Layla said. "I promised the nurse looking after my clients while I'm gone that I would go with her on her next set of rounds and help her get to know the patients. Plus, I have a lot of reports I need to do before we go on our honeymoon. If Andrew says he's good and he's willing to do our music, I'm fine with that."

The look Andrew gave Layla warmed his heart. He was surprised by the yearning it created in him, but also by the way it made him wish that Allie would know a love like that.

Andrew turned his gaze to him. "I would love for you to play at our wedding. Could we say yes temporarily? I'd like to talk to Allie about it first. She's been through a lot the past couple of weeks. And I don't want to add to her burden."

"I agree," Layla said. "The last thing I want to do is hurt Allie."

Enid stepped forward. "You let me take care of her. Yes, she's hurting, but the only way to deal with your hurt is to face it. In a town this size, she can't avoid Cole forever. Nor should she want to."

Then she turned and looked at him. "You've been a good friend to Andrew. I won't pretend to know about all your shenanigans, but I do know enough to say it would be special to have you a part of the celebration. Allie can handle it, even if she doesn't know it yet."

It felt good to have Enid's support. Growing up, he was never sure if Enid loved him or hated him. Andrew used to say that was just her way, but he had never been sure. He just wished he knew it would be all right with Allie.

"Well doesn't that just figure," Mary said. "It's always about Allison. When is the world going to stop revolving around her? If she ruins one more family event..."

Mary shook her head like she had more to say but had thought better of it.

"Allie has never ruined anything," Enid said, glaring at Mary. "The only ruined family events where Allie has been involved were because of your constant picking on her. I've held my tongue because Layla says that all this negativity is bad for my health. But if I have to have a heart attack and die to make you see how unfair you're being to your daughter, then so be it. She is a wonderful young woman, and I don't suppose I've told her that often enough. I don't tell people the good things I see in them often enough, but thanks to the healthy-living groups and the new Bible studies I'm part of here at this church, I know I need to do better job of it."

Clearly a lot of things had changed at Arcadia Valley Community Church since Cole had last been here. But he was glad for those changes, especially if it meant one of the crankiest old women in town was learning to love others.

"Clearly that weird cleanse you're on has made you crazier than ever," Mary said. "My biggest regret in life is letting my children stay with you when we moved. Thanks to you, my daughter has become a person I'm ashamed of. She can improve her looks with a little makeup and a decent hairstyle, and had she been given proper encouragement to better herself and do something with her life, she wouldn't be shacking up with some homeless man because she finally got fired for her inappropriate behavior."

Cole had never wanted to hit a woman in his entire life. But Mary's words almost changed his mind.

Enid stepped forward and looked Mary in the eye. "We have all told you that Wade is not a homeless man. He's a friend of the family with an empty house Allie is staying in. And the only good I can see in you is that you let the kids stay with me. Otherwise, I don't know that they would have a lick of human decency in their bodies. I repeat what I said about Allie being a wonderful human being. I can't say the same for you, or, God help me, my son. I know I made a lot of mistakes raising my children, but somehow the good Lord gave me enough goodness to do right by my grandchildren."

Shaking her head, Enid turned and looked at Andrew. "And that goes for you and your cousin Caroline as well. You're a good man, and I'm proud to know you."

Nothing could have prepared Cole for this level of drama, but as he watched the two women square off, he could understand why Allie had been so stressed in their recent interactions. Living with this would be enough to make even the most sane person go crazy.

"Thanks, Gram." Andrew held out his arms, and his grandmother stepped into them.

Tears came to Cole's eyes as he saw the love between them. At least Allie had this in her life. He was glad to see that both Andrew and Allie had found a better place in their relationships with their grandmother. In high school, Enid had been something of an embarrassment. Back then, she dressed like a hippie, which everyone thought was silly. She still dressed the same way now, but at least it was now cool to express individuality through weird clothes.

Plus, over the years, Enid had mellowed considerably.

"You've turned my children against me, that's what you've done," Mary said. "I hate you for it."

Still holding his grandmother in his arms, Andrew looked over at his mother. "You did that all on your own. If you're so worried about drama with Allie, then perhaps you shouldn't start it. I'm doing my best to have a relationship with you and Dad, but it's hard for me when you're constantly attacking the two people I love most in the world besides my fiancée. Maybe, when we leave, you should stay behind and talk to the pastor about reconciliation and what that actually means. I know you're not a believer, so if you don't like his answer, then I'm sure he can give you a recommendation for a good counselor."

The anger on Mary's face was evident, and as she opened her mouth to speak, Andrew held up his hand. "No. I'm done. The only person with the potential to ruin my wedding is you. My only regret is not saying something sooner. Even though it's not a good excuse, I can only say that I've been so busy taking classes for my counseling degree, helping on the farm and trying to make peace happen among the members of my family, I missed what that peace is costing the people most important to me. Layla and I both want close relationships with all of our family members. But we're breaking under the weight of trying to make everyone else happy. This is why Caroline and Hayden eloped."

Though Andrew's words were meant to help his mother see the truth, Cole realized that he could apply those words to his own life. Especially his relationship with Allie. He'd nearly killed himself trying to make her happy back in high school. It hadn't worked. But what would it have been like if he'd focused on his own happiness?

One of the crazy things about Allie was that he had always admired her for the fact that she wasn't consumed with other people's thoughts. She wore what she wanted, did what she wanted, and didn't seem to care whether people liked it or not. Listening to the argument between Enid and Mary, Cole could see how that was all Enid's influence. And yet, Cole had missed the part of Allie that had been humiliated by the attention she got because of Cole's crush.

More things to think about, and to figure out how he could apply them in moving forward with his life.

Andrew turned to Cole. "I'm sorry that you and the pastor had to get caught up in the family drama. I know you already feel stuck in the middle with Allie."

"Don't be sorry. You're a good friend, and I meant what I said about being willing to support you however I could. I'm here for you. And even though I'm somewhat of an outsider, you made me realize a lot of things I need to do differently in my own life."

Layla smiled at him, then at her fiancé. "I'm glad. And I'm especially glad that you're here in time to join us in celebrating our marriage. What we want most is for the people closest to us to share in our joy and hold us accountable through the years, especially when times get tough. We're not so naïve as to think things won't get tough, but they will be easier because of people like you."

"Well said." Uncle Vince came around his desk. "I think we've all been given plenty to think about here today, so why don't we take a break for now? Andrew, if there's anything you need for your wedding, don't hesitate to ask. Mary, if you would like to continue this conversation at some point, my door is always open. I'm also happy to recommend a number of different interfaith counselors with spiritual leanings that more accurately reflect your own."

He gestured to the door, and as everyone started filing out, Enid said, "what about me? You didn't invite me to seek your help."

Uncle Vince laughed. "Enid, I know that, invited or not, you'll always be here to tell me exactly what's on your mind."

Everyone, including Enid, joined in the laughter. Except Mary, who still wore a sour expression on her face.

"I have to keep everyone on their toes. Now, if you would just eat those prune cookies I made you instead of throwing them out, I'm sure we'd see great improvement in the quality of your sermons."

They might be seeing a kinder, gentler Enid, but it was clear that some things about the old woman would never change.

For the first time since Allie's final rejection of him after her accident, Cole felt like he had truly come home. And even though he had been thrust directly into the middle of Bigby family craziness, it had given him the opportunity to remember why he loved these people.

Enid was crazy, yes, but she could always be counted on to take care of others and do the right thing. That compassion was reflected in Andrew and Allie, as was Enid's attitude and desire to walk to the beat of her own drum. They didn't have the same drums as Enid, that was the point. It was just too bad Mary didn't see that.

He was disappointed to see that Mary left with everyone else. But hopefully, she would be back.

Once everyone left, Cole sank into one of the chairs at

Uncle Vince's desk. "Wow, that was intense," he said, sighing. "Is this what you deal with on a regular basis?"

Uncle Vince chuckled. "Different families have different dramas. No family is without their problems. But I find it to be a great pleasure and a great joy to help them work through them. The biggest reason I love your Aunt Helen is not that things have always been perfect between us. But because we've had the strength to work through the hardest moments and love each other even when it seemed impossible. That is truly what love is."

His uncle's words made him realize just how shallow his previous feelings for Allie were. Since the car accident, he had slowly been letting go of his attachment to her. And now, he could see her as a wonderful woman who deserved a great deal of happiness, but he no longer needed to be part of it. Still, she would remain in his prayers, and he hoped God would give her strength and comfort as she dealt with a difficult situation. If he could help her in any way, he would be happy to, as he would help anyone in need.

He just wasn't determined to be her hero anymore.

## 9

The morning of Andrew's wedding, Allie woke up covered in hives. Every inch of her skin felt like it was on fire. At least the Mexican-style bridesmaid dress hanging in her closet had been made with winter in mind and would cover most of it. But her face... That was the real problem. If there were words to describe uglier than ugly, that would be a kinder description than what her face looked like.

Even after she'd enlisted Jess's expertise in makeup, she still looked terrible. Worse, when she arrived at the church, she was five minutes late. No one else would notice, but as she trudged up the steps, she dreaded the fact that she would have to face her mother.

"Is this your idea of a joke?" her mother asked as soon as Allie entered the church.

"No," she muttered. "I've tried every remedy I know. But I'm covered in them."

"Covered in what?

If Allie's messed-up face wasn't what her mother was

86

talking about, she wasn't sure she wanted to know the rest of her mother's complaints.

"Hives."

Her mother stared at her, and after a few minutes, she stepped back. "How do you know they're hives and not some infectious disease you caught from the homeless man you're with?"

After two weeks, her mother still bought into this ridiculous theory?

"I would explain to you again that I'm not living with a homeless man, but I don't know how to do so in a way that you understand any differently than I have the past several times. However, I know what this is. I break out in hives whenever I'm under an extreme amount of stress. This has happened before, and the doctor told me that it will go away on its own."

"I don't appreciate your tone of voice," her mother said icily. "Have you seen a doctor today?"

"It's Christmas Eve. Everything is closed. I'm also pretty sure that because I don't have a job anymore, I also don't have insurance."

Her mother glared at her. "Once again, you're only thinking about yourself. Whose fault is it that you don't have a job or insurance? You would risk infecting everyone at this wedding because you're too proud to see a doctor?"

Allie tried to remain calm. She even sent a small but desperate plea to God to please help her control her temper in the situation.

"The doctors are closed today, so even if I went to see them, no one would be available."

"You could go to the emergency room. It's open 24/7. You could have been there and back with all the time you've been wasting. Look at that makeup job. I realize that you think makeup is silly and vain, but the least you could have done is make an effort to look nice for your brother's wedding, instead of like a toddler who'd gotten into her mother's lipstick."

It was futile to tell her mother that Jess, who had once worked as a makeup artist, had spent the past hour on Allie's makeup. But she was saved from having to figure out something to say when Jess walked in.

"I did the best I could with what I had," Jess said. "The splotches on her face didn't make it easy, and I don't think there's a concealer in the world strong enough to cover up hives. Honestly, I think it would be better if she didn't wear makeup."

Jess hadn't had the pleasure of too many interactions with Allie's mother. But she was about to enter the hurricane at full force.

"And just who are you?"

Jess stuck out her hand. "Jess Anderson. Former makeup artist to the stars. Now, regular housewife and best friend to Allie."

"At least now I understand the ridiculousness."

The church door opened again, and Cole walked in with his brother, carrying Caitlin.

"The wedding isn't due to begin for two hours," Allie's mother said, sounding even more annoyed.

"I'm doing the music, and my brother and his wife are here to help decorate." Cole's voice was smooth and pleasant, and Allie wished she had that level of composure.

Since her talk with Gram, she'd been praying for Cole, praying for God's blessing on him, and praying that she could find a way to love him the way God did. When Gram told her that Cole was doing the music, Allie had been surprised to find that the old irritation hadn't welled up the way it used to. Of course, now she was covered with hives.

Funny how she hadn't realized until now that her first bout of hives, which the doctor said was stress related, had been opening night of the school play, in which she had the lead role. Cole had spent the entire week leading up to the play telling her how much he believed in her and how he thought she was going to do such a wonderful job, and how he couldn't wait to cheer her on. She'd been dreading what would happen at the play.

But she couldn't really blame the hives on Cole. She had to learn to stop being so nervous over her fears of what he might do or what might happen. She'd thought she'd been trying, and she certainly had been praying enough to prove it. But she must've done something wrong, or not said the right things, or not prayed hard enough. Because here it was, her brother's big day, and Allie looked like she'd lost a fight with a wasp's nest.

Allie's mother turned back to Jess. "Well since you made her look so ridiculous, you're going to have to fix it. And, since you say you're her best friend, you can take her to the emergency room to make sure no one is going to catch whatever horrible disease she has. Just make sure she's back in time for the wedding."

"Are we being punked?" James asked, looking around.

"I don't know what that is, and I don't appreciate that tone of voice. My son is getting married, and I will not have his wedding ruined by all this nonsense. Allison, go see a doctor before you infect all of us."

Great. So now everyone was going to think something was wrong with her. Well, there was. But it wasn't anything anyone could catch.

She looked over at Jess, hoping her friend would at least

play along with the ridiculousness. But before Allie could come up with a plan, Cole stepped forward.

"I'll take her. Jess doesn't need to be sitting around in an emergency room with a bunch of sick people in her condition."

Allie stared at him. Jess hadn't yet told James about the baby. She'd told Allie that she finally came up with the perfect way to tell him, and it was happening soon. There was no way she would have told Cole.

Which meant despite Cole's promise to her, he'd just let it slip.

And of course, James picked up on it right away. "What condition?"

Jess looked like she wanted to kill someone. Preferably, two someones.

"She's a mother with a nursing baby," Allie said. "Anything she catches will be passed on to Caitlin."

James looked over at Cole like he wasn't buying Allie's explanation. "Is that what you meant?"

"No," Cole said. "I know I promised Allie I wouldn't say anything, but Allie accidentally told me that Jess is pregnant again. I don't know why she hasn't told you yet, but based on your question, I think you suspect anyway."

Jess made a noise, and tears started streaming down her face. "You promised," she said, as she ran out of the room.

"I'll go talk to her," James said. "I can't believe she told you before she told me."

He followed, carrying Caitlin, leaving Allie alone with Cole and her mother.

"Once again, you've ruined someone's happiness by making their news all about you. I hope all the misery you cause is worth it," her mother said.

"That's enough," Cole said. "I haven't heard you say a

single nice thing about your daughter. I can't believe a mother has so little affection for her child. I wish you could see what a wonderful person she is. Honestly, this is all my fault. I let it slip, and then when she gave a perfectly reasonable explanation for my words, I went ahead and ruined it."

He turned and looked at Allie, and though she knew he meant well, she also knew that his words didn't make a difference. And wasn't that how it always went with Allie and Cole.

"How dare you criticize me. You know nothing about me. You're just like her, trying to draw attention away from yourself and your indiscretions instead of facing up to them. I suggest you hurry and get her seen by a doctor so this wedding isn't further destroyed."

The expression on his face told Allie that he was going to come up with some other retort. But that would make matters worse. And right now, she didn't have the strength to deal with worse.

She grabbed him by the arm and tugged him toward the door. "The faster we get to a doctor, the faster we can get back in time for the wedding."

"But she said-"

"It doesn't matter. I've been hearing it my whole life. Let's not give her any more ammunition. If we are one second late for the wedding, she will blame it all on the fact that we spent too much time arguing now."

Her mother gave a snort. "Fine time for you to be listening to me."

Despite Allie's own words, she turned to look back at her mother. "Do you want me to listen to you or not? No matter what I do, it's wrong. I'll see you when I get back from the doctor."

It was ridiculous for Allie to have to waste her money on

an emergency room visit when she already knew what was wrong. As Allie followed Cole to his truck, it was tempting to tell him to just drive around for a while, but she knew that if she faked going to the ER, her mother would find out somehow.

"Do you really think it's nothing?" Cole asked as they got into his truck.

He hadn't been there for her earlier explanation of her hives, and it didn't seem right to let him know the connection. Not when he was honestly trying to do the right thing.

"It's just hives. I've had them before. She's overreacting, but if I don't get it looked at, I'll never hear the end of it."

He gave her a sympathetic look. "Do Andrew and Layla know what's going on?"

"No," she said. "They have enough to deal with, with all the wedding stuff going on. I know it's nothing, and given that Layla is a nurse, she'll look at it and say it's nothing, but it's not worth causing them aggravation on their special day. Whatever time they spend mediating between me and my mother will be less time they have for getting ready, taking pictures, doing all the other stuff people do before their wedding. That's not fair."

The look of understanding he gave her made her feel better about her decision. But it didn't mean she and Cole could be friends.

After all, they still hadn't dealt with the fact that he had just given up the secret he'd been entrusted with.

"I'm still mad at you for revealing Jess's pregnancy," she said, looking over at Cole.

"I know," he said. "Not my best move. But I really didn't want her going to the ER and risking getting sick with something that could hurt the baby."

She sighed. "Your heart was in the right place. And if I

hadn't told you to begin with, we wouldn't be in this situation."

The trouble with being mad at Cole for so many of the things she was mad at him for was that she had always played a role in the situation. Could she blame him for the first time she'd gotten hives? Yes. But it was also her fault for not knowing how to handle the stress. Could she be mad at him for all the times she'd gotten in trouble in school because of Cole? Yes. Though maybe if Allie had found more positive ways to respond to him, maybe she wouldn't have.

"I know, but I still feel responsible." As they turned onto the main road leading to the hospital, Cole looked over at her. "I was praying about the situation the other day, and I remember the time in high school when I hadn't seen you at lunch, so I was worried about you. I searched through the whole school, afraid you might be in trouble or something. When I found you hiding in the janitor's closet, you yelled at me and told me you hated me and to leave you alone. One of the teachers heard you, and you got in trouble for being there in the first place. It occurred to me when I was praying, you were hiding from me, weren't you?"

The sadness on Cole's face made her feel bad for nodding. But it was true. But maybe, if they spoke to one another honestly with the intention of understanding, maybe they could find a way to that forgiveness Gram had spoken about.

"That morning, you told me you had a special surprise for me. I hadn't liked any of your other surprises, like when you sang to me in the middle of the pep rally, or when you decorated my locker with all those embarrassing pictures of me, or that giant stuffed dog you gave me for Valentine's Day that I had to lug everywhere because it was too big to fit in my locker. So, I thought if I found a good place to hide, you wouldn't be able to find me and humiliate me. But it didn't work out that way. It never did."

As Allie thought about all the ways she'd tried to avoid humiliation, she had to admit that none of them ever worked. It seemed like hiding only ever made everything worse. That was probably also true with her parents. They would start in on her, she would hide, and when they found her, they had more reasons to be angry with her.

"I'm sorry for getting you in trouble that day," Cole said. "And I'm sorry for making you feel so humiliated that you felt like you had to hide. I didn't realize that you'd interpret my actions as humiliation. I thought they'd make you see how much I loved you."

Allie looked sideways at him. "How is a picture of me as a baby with a naked butt not humiliating?"

"I thought it was cute. Don't girls think naked babies are cute?"

"Not when it's your butt, and you're in high school. How would you feel if someone posted a picture of your butt on your locker?"

Cole made a noise. "Sorry. I guess I hadn't thought of it that way before. But in my defense, you've always had a pretty cute butt. Mine, not so much."

"Gross. I don't want to think about your butt. Where did you get that picture, anyway?"

Cole's groan made her smile. "I was hoping you wouldn't ask. But in the spirit of being honest, I took a picture of the one your grandmother had on her refrigerator. Not that it's an excuse, but I figured since it was on the fridge, you must not mind people seeing it."

It was Allie's turn to groan. "Ugh. I hated that picture. It made me too embarrassed to ever invite friends over. I was so glad when she got into feng shui and her book told her that having our pictures on her refrigerator was putting bad energy into the house."

"We've had a lot of misunderstandings between us, haven't we? I wish we hadn't been so scared to honestly share our feelings the way we are now."

He looked so earnest it seemed almost cruel to point out the truth.

"A lot of it has been misunderstanding," Allie said, able to agree to that part. "But if we had been honest with one another, I would have told you point blank that I didn't like you. I tried to do it in a nice way. A number of times. But you never believed me."

At least he didn't look crushed by her words. In some ways, his calm response made her feel safer. So many times, when she'd been honest with her mother about her feelings, her mother would go off the handle and scream at her, much like how she'd done in the church.

"You're right. When I asked Andrew why he'd never told me that you didn't like me, he said he had, but I'd never listened. I'm really sorry for not listening to you and respecting your wishes. But I have to ask, was your dislike of me a flaw in my character, or just because I pursued you too hard?"

She had never thought about that question before. Why does anyone dislike another person? Why did her mother dislike her so much? Was her mother's inability to love her a flaw in Allie, a flaw in her mother, or combination of both? She'd spent years agonizing over the answer to that question. She wondered if it had been the same for Cole.

"I'm not sure," she said finally. "At first, you were just a stupid friend of my brother's. Because honestly, that's how I felt about all of his friends. Sibling rivalry, you know. So, I guess it wasn't you on a personal level, because I never took the time to know you. That said, what kind of person chases after a girl who's made it clear she doesn't want to be with him?"

"I'd like to think he was a dreamer, but listening to you, I would say he was a stalker. Wow. Who knew that's what I was. I could say I'm sorry to you a million times, and it still wouldn't adequately express how terrible I feel at what I did to you. Why didn't you tell anyone?"

They parked at the emergency room and started toward the door.

"I did. But everyone thought what you were doing was cute, or that I was overreacting. And you never did anything dangerous. It wasn't like I'd wake up in the middle of the night and you'd be there, staring at me. You never made me feel unsafe on a physical level. I don't think anyone saw it as a problem."

He opened the door for her, allowing her to go first. There was no one at the desk, and as she reached for the button to call a nurse, he looked at her in a way he had never looked at her before.

"I want you to know that I heard everything you said to me today. What I did was wrong, and you need to know that. I take full responsibility for my actions, and I can see where I made your high school life miserable. I'm so very sorry."

He reached forward and pushed the nurse call button. "I brought you here only because I don't want to cause any further trouble for your brother's wedding. I had no ulterior motive, and I promise I will leave you alone in the future."

When the nurse entered, he went to sit in one of the waiting-room chairs. He picked up a magazine, and started thumbing through it, leaving Allie to talk to the nurse.

The nurse took her information, and while it felt good to

have her privacy, she also somewhat missed Cole's presence. Their conversation had felt good to her, mostly because it was one of the first conversations she'd had in a long time where the other person was seeking to understand her, not judging her, or trying to tell her how to live her life. Even the people she thought were on her side, like Gram and Andrew, didn't listen so much as give her advice. Good advice but, nonetheless, what she really needed was someone to just listen.

But would encouraging Cole make him think she was open to something more? Because while she thought she might be open to having him as a friend, she didn't think she could handle the rest.

## 10

_____

No one should have to spend Christmas Eve in the emergency room. But here Cole was, waiting for Allie to come out. A young family had come in with their little one being treated for a burn because he'd gotten too close to the wood stove. And now, another woman was walking through the door, trying to soothe an inconsolable baby, and tugging two unruly children behind her.

When the nurse checked her in, the woman started to go toward the back, but the nurse stopped her.

"They have to stay here. This is a hospital, not the daycare."

"But I don't have anyone to watch them, and the baby is sick. Surely you can make an exception."

The nurse shook her head. "Children under twelve are not allowed. It's for their safety. You wouldn't want to get them sick from being exposed to the other patients, now would you? But I'll go back and see what we can do."

Sighing, the woman looked over at the play area as the

nurse left the room. Before she could say anything, her phone rang.

"I know. But I'm at the emergency room with my daughter and she's sick. I can't-"

Whatever the person on the other end said, it made tears stream down the woman's face. "I understand. You do what you have to do."

Cole got up and walked over to the woman. "Look, I know you don't know me from Adam, but I'll watch your kids when you take your baby back."

He pulled out his wallet, and handed it to her. "I'm Cole Anderson. That's my ID right there. As you can see, it looks just like me. You keep my wallet with you."

"I know who you are," the woman said, holding out her hand. "Emily Locke, but you knew me in school as Emily Cunningham. I'm friends with Allie Bigby. So, I know you're crazy but harmless. Thanks for being willing to watch the kids. The boy is Jacob, and the girl is Jasmine. But she only answers to Princess Jasmine, and if they ask you to buy anything from the vending machine, the answer is no. I'm sure they've got to have a water fountain around here somewhere, and they just had supper."

She started to sit in a nearby seat to wait for the nurse to return, but then she paused. "What are you doing here, anyway?"

From the way Emily spoke about knowing him, he wasn't sure how she was going to react to what he had to say. But he'd been the one to act so crazy, so he had to live with the consequences.

"Allie broke out in hives, and her brother's wedding is in..." Cole looked at the clock on the wall. "A little over an hour. She's supposed to be a bridesmaid, but her mother was worried that she had some kind of horrible disease and would make everyone sick. So, we're here, getting the all clear for Allie to go forward in the wedding."

"Were you the one who made her break out in hives?" Emily asked, giving a half snort, half giggle.

"Probably." Cole sighed. "But I'm sure her mother also had a lot to do with it."

Emily nodded. "That family is all kinds of messed up, and it's a wonder Allie can stay sane. And be a decent human being. Had she not gotten fired, she was going to work Christmas for me, so I could be home with my kids. I'd forgotten that her brother was getting married Christmas Eve, so it's pretty amazing that she'd be willing to come in the day after such a special event, and on Christmas no less, so I could be with my family. Of course, with Allie gone, they were making me work today and tomorrow. But since my boss just fired me for choosing to take my daughter to the emergency room instead of coming to work, I guess I'll be home for Christmas after all."

As Emily turned her gaze to her children, she shook her head. "I try so hard to give them a good life, but it seems like life keeps kicking me while I'm down."

She looked like she had something else to say, but then the baby, who'd stopped fussing for a moment, started to wail again. "Her fever is just so high. I've never seen anything like it."

Cole didn't know what to say in response. The only baby he'd ever been around was Caitlin. And she'd never been sick, just cranky over teething and diaper rash.

His phone beeped, indicating an incoming text.

*Where are you? Have you heard from Allie? Mom says she's off being Allison, but that tells me nothing.*

Why had it been so hard for Mary to explain what was going on? She'd been so concerned about ruining Andrew's wedding, but she was the one causing trouble for failing to communicate.

*At the ER with Allie. She woke up with hives. Nothing serious. Mary threw a fit and made her go.*

The good thing about texting was that Cole could be blunt without sounding rude. Because right now, he had nothing but rude things to say.

*Is she okay?*

How was Cole supposed to answer that? He wanted to say yes, because he thought Allie was probably all right. But what if she wasn't?

*As far as I know. Waiting to hear from doctor.*

The response came almost right away. *Layla says we'll be there soon.*

Allie was going to kill him.

*Please don't. If anything holds up your wedding, your mother will blame Allie, and Allie will be crushed.*

The lack of response on the other end made Cole think that Andrew and Layla were discussing what would happen next.

*My sister is more important to us.*

He closed his eyes and shoved his phone back in his pocket. Allie was so lucky to have the love of a brother like Andrew. He just hoped that she would forgive him when Andrew showed up. Mary might blame Allie for all the family drama, but she did everything she could to avoid it.

"Everything okay?" Emily asked.

"It will be," he said.

The nurse came out, and he looked in Emily's direction. "You go make sure your baby is going to be okay, and I'll make sure these two are."

"You're sure? I don't know how long we'll be, and I would hate for you to miss Andrew's wedding."

"I can't leave until Allie does, and it sounds like Andrew is on his way. It'll all work out."

Emily whistled. "Sounds more like thermonuclear war is about to happen. I'm glad I'll be in the back with the doctors. But I like your optimism."

Though he would readily agree to Emily's assessment, saying so wasn't going to help anyone. He turned his attention back to her children, who seemed content playing with the toys in the children's area.

A short while later, Andrew and Layla entered the ER, wearing their wedding finery.

"Any word on Allie?" Andrew asked.

Cole shook his head. "I think no news is good news. She said this has happened before, when she was dealing with a lot of stress."

His words didn't erase the concern from her brother's face.

Looking concerned, Andrew said, "But Allie didn't have to go to the hospital. This sounds more serious than that."

"Only because your mother insisted that she make sure it wasn't something contagious that was going to ruin your wedding."

"Argh," Layla said. "The only person ruining our wedding is her. Why didn't she have me look at her? I could have told her if it was serious enough for the emergency room."

As much as he hated the blame game, it was important for them to understand that none of this was Allie's fault. "Because Mary insisted that she stay away from you and not infect the bride."

Layla let out a long sigh. "Allie's certain it's hives from stress?"

"As certain as someone who's had it can be. But she's not a doctor, so I suppose this is the safest route."

He watched Layla's face as she appeared to consider this information.

"I'm going to see if they'll let me go back and talk to her," Layla said, walking to the main desk and pushing the button.

When the nurse came out, Layla spoke with her quietly, and he couldn't hear what was being said. But after a brief exchange, Layla followed her back.

Andrew slumped into the chair next to Cole. "Caroline and Hayden were right to elope. I wish we had, except then I wouldn't have been able to see Layla in that dress."

Then Andrew grinned. "Doesn't she look amazing? I'm telling you, I cannot believe what a beautiful woman she is. Both inside and out, but wow. The sight of her in that dress blows me away."

"Isn't it bad luck to see the bride in her dress before the wedding?"

"It's worse luck to have a wedding without the people who mean the most to you standing next to you over a stupid technicality. If Allie is not there, we're postponing the wedding until she can be."

"Oh no, you're not." Mary's distinctive voice rang through the ER. "Why are you letting her ruin everything? This is just more of Allison's need for attention."

Was she seriously still playing that card?

Cole turned and saw Bart, Andrew and Allie's father, coming in behind her.

"She'd better be dying, to pull a stunt like this," Bart said.

How could a family be so unfeeling? Cole stood and

looked at him. "The only reason she's here is because your wife insisted."

"But I'm not going to let her get everyone else sick," Mary said. "It's just like her, coming down with some kind of skin disease right before the wedding, and ruining all of our pictures."

Andrew stood as well. "No one gets sick on purpose. That's just ridiculous. I'm sure she didn't want any of this to happen. Why are you still being so hard on her?"

He'd already made his thoughts clear at the church. It was sad to see that Andrew's mother still didn't respect his wishes on the wedding she seemed to so desperately want and was afraid of being ruined.

"And why do you keep defending her?" Mary's voice was shrill, and Cole noticed that the children had stopped playing and were watching them. At least no one else was in the ER.

"Because I'm all she has," Andrew said. "And you know what? I gave you the chance to do the right thing, but you chose differently. My wedding will happen when it happens, and I respectfully ask that you not be a part of it. And don't you dare blame Allie for this, because she has no idea that I had asked you to back off."

The back doors to the ER opened, and Allie walked out with Layla.

"Don't do this," Allie said. "The doctor says I'm fine, and that it was just stress. We have thirty minutes until the wedding, plenty of time to get back to the church and for the ceremony to continue as planned. Mom, Dad, I'm sorry I'm such a disappointment to you. But we need to find a way to stop being so hateful to one another so Andrew and Layla don't always feel like they're in the middle."

She turned and smiled at Cole. "I talked to Emily back

there while we were waiting for the doctor to see the baby. Thanks for being willing to look out for her. She's had a hard go of it, and I don't know how she does it."

Cole was impressed how even in the middle of a personal crisis, she had still found it in her heart to be there for a friend. Allie looked over at her brother.

"If you can help me get the kids' car seats into your car, I'd appreciate it. Cole doesn't have enough seatbelts, and it looks like Emily is going to be here a while."

"Overnight," Layla said, sighing. "At least from the sounds of that baby's breathing. Allie has watched the kids before, so she told Emily she'd be willing to keep them overnight. I talked to my Quintana cousins, and they said they'd watch the kids during the ceremony so Allie could stand up with us, and Cole could handle the music. Sometimes it takes a village, and there's no better place than Arcadia Valley for taking care of their own."

Mary gave a very unladylike snort. "You've got to be kidding me."

"Nope," Andrew said. "This is exactly why I love this town, why I choose to live here, and why I'm grateful the woman I love calls this place home."

Any thought he might have had about not staying in Arcadia Valley disappeared at Andrew's words. Andrew was exactly right. Cole had been all over the world and never known the level of caring this community had for one another.

The party set out for the church, and he was disappointed that Allie chose to ride with her brother. But it made sense, considering the children needed to be in the car with the car seats. Which left Cole to chauffer the bride to her wedding.

Layla was indeed a beautiful woman, especially in her

wedding gown. He wasn't up on the latest fashions, or any fashion for that matter, but the Mexican design was clearly hand-sewn, and probably antique.

"I'm sure you never expected to be driven to your wedding in a beat-up old truck," he said, trying to lighten the mood.

"As long as I marry Andrew today, I don't care. I'd have married him in the ER if I'd had to."

The smile she gave him made him happy that his friend was marrying someone who loved him that much. Maybe that's what had been wrong with his crush on Allie all these years. She'd never loved him like that, and he knew that he deserved such a deep love.

Layla's expression softened. "I'm sorry you got stuck in the middle of all the family drama. Thanks for being there for Allie. She's a good woman, and I know it probably horrified her to be thrust into all of this turmoil."

"I just hope her hives aren't that bad." Cole looked over at Layla. "She was right about that, wasn't she? I can't imagine Emily what have let her take her kids if she had anything contagious."

For a moment, Cole wasn't sure Layla was going to tell him. "Of course, she was right. I hate it when people self-diagnose and don't get a professional opinion. But Allie is a smart woman, and I'm sure she would have sought medical help if it was warranted. She'll be fine. I just wish Mary would give her some breathing space. What Allie really needs is a break from all the stress. Between losing her job, her car accident, all the family drama, and your return, it's a lot to handle." Layla looked at him sideways.

"Sorry, but it's true. And if it helps, I don't think you've ever meant her any harm. Under any other circumstances, I think your return would have barely been a blip on her stress radar."

Cole wasn't sure what he was supposed to say to that, but it was nice to know that someone was on his side- sort of.

"So, if Andrew has seemed distant, be patient. He's doing the best he can to keep family members from killing each other, while helping Allie to stay sane. And that's on top of his schoolwork and all the wedding madness. I just wanted you to know that he still sees you as a good friend, and I hope none of this affects your friendship."

Once again, Cole couldn't help feeling that Andrew had struck gold in marrying Layla. So many times when guys got married their wives felt threatened by their friendships, and pretty soon, the old buddy was no more. He'd seen it often enough in the Army, and while he hadn't expected to come home to find all of his friendships unchanged, it was nice to see he could still pick up with his friends where they'd left off.

"Thank you. If there is anything I can do to make the situation easier on Andrew, don't hesitate to ask. You're right that I never meant Allie any harm. The few times we've spoken since coming back, I realized what a grave disservice I was doing her. And me. We both deserve the same kind of love and happiness that you and Andrew have. Whether that be with each other, or not."

Layla's smile warmed his heart. "We all deserve this kind of love and happiness. I pray you'll find it."

They arrived at the church, and Cole helped her out of his beat-up truck, careful not to let her dress touch the dirty exterior. He hadn't washed it because snow was in the forecast, and the scent on the breeze told him the weatherman had been correct. As if to confirm his nose, a few stray snowflakes danced on the air.

"I think it's snowing," Cole said. "Maybe we'll have a white Christmas after all."

Layla gave him another smile. "I hope so. I told Andrew that the most perfect thing for our wedding would be a light dusting of snow."

She lifted the bottom of her dress to reveal white snow boots.

"And I do love a happy ending." Then she leaned in and gave him a quick hug. "I'll be praying for yours. Even if Andrew hadn't told me what a great guy you were, I can still tell. Don't lose hope. I just know God has something wonderful planned for you."

**11**

T he rest of the wedding went exactly as planned. The good thing about going to the emergency room, was that Allie had gotten some medication to help ease the itching. Normally she wouldn't have taken it without researching all the side effects and weighing the risks. But for Andrew's wedding, she went ahead and took the medicine.

The meds still left her splotchy, but at least she hadn't stood at the front of the church itching like a mad woman.

So here it was, Christmas morning, just before dawn, and she was sitting at the kitchen table at Wade's house, drinking coffee, watching the snow gently drift across the farmland. People had thought she was crazy for spending all that money on a greenhouse for her lavender, but it was nice to know that even in this weather, production continued.

She smiled as she opened her email on her phone again and read the message from Nyssa's Naturals, an up-and-coming natural beauty company, inviting her to come to their headquarters in Oregon to showcase her products in the new year. If they liked what they saw, all of her financial problems would be over.

Imagine, her products being featured in a number of popular regional boutiques. Of course, she'd have to increase production, but the thing that had always stood in the way was her job. Without a job, she had had plenty of time to resupply her dwindling stock. Perhaps, if this deal went through, she could even hire some people, like Emily, and give them a chance to better themselves. That had always been her hope. Not just finding success for herself, but being able to help others.

The sun was starting to rise, and Emily should be arriving soon. She'd texted Allie to let her know the baby was doing much better, but would need to remain in the hospital for a few days. However, Emily wanted to at least bring by the children's Christmas presents and spend a few moments with her older children while the baby slept.

She busied herself making whole wheat pancakes so they could all start the day with a healthy breakfast. She'd ground the wheat berries herself, a task she used to enjoy doing, but as her job got busier, she hadn't had the time for a luxury such as homemade pancakes made completely from scratch. The eggs were fresh from Bigby Farm, and their bright yellow yolks were the color of sunshine, her very favorite color other than lavender. Something inside Allie told her that today was going to be a great day.

Maybe it was because, as the Bible said, every day was a new beginning. This afternoon, she would take the children over to Bigby Farm for the family celebration. And even though she'd be forced to face her mother and the various aunts and uncles- and deal with their unkind remarks- she knew it was going to be all right.

Her phone *dinged*, and she went to check it, in case it was

Emily. With a sigh, she realized too late it was simply an incoming email. One of these days, she was going to have to figure out which *beep* went with what, and how to turn off the ones she didn't want. Right now, it seemed to be all or nothing.

But when she glanced at the subject, she was glad she'd checked.

After talking to Gram about all of her regrets, Allie had started searching online for her late uncle's daughter. Most of her attempts hadn't gotten her very far, but Bigby wasn't a very common last name.

*RE: Adam Bigby*

*Your message was unexpected. I spoke with my mother, who confirmed that my grandmother is indeed Enid Bigby. However, my mother is concerned about Enid's mental state. Apparently, that's why, after my father's passing, she chose to cut off all ties to the Bigbys. But I think it's sweet that you are helping your grandmother in her old age. I don't know if I want to meet her or not, but I would like to continue talking to you to find out if it's worth pursuing. I have my own family to think of, and I don't wish to put them in the middle of drama we didn't ask for. I'm married with two children, and they are my primary concern.*

*I wish you a Merry Christmas, and I will be in touch soon.*

*Madison Bigby McKay*

IF EVER THERE was a Christmas wish Allie had most desperately wanted to come true, this would be it. Gram was going to be so happy when she learned that she had found Madison. True, Madison had expressed concern over Gram's sanity, but the door was open. As long as she could convince Madison that Gram wasn't nuts.

A knock sounded at the door, and she got up to answer it. It was Emily, laden with packages, and looking exhausted.

"Did you get any sleep at all?"

Emily shook her head. "The nurses were in and out all night checking on Jennifer."

"I've got breakfast made. I'm sure you haven't eaten. Help yourself, and I'll get these presents under the tree. I can't believe the kids are still asleep, but last night was crazy for everyone."

"I hope you didn't get the tree just for my family," Emily said, looking around at the festive living room.

Twinkling lights were strewn across the room, and decorations were scattered about. The tree was a small one, but it was full of ornaments and lights, just the way Allie liked it.

"Not at all. Gram's house looks like a wedding threw up all over the inside of it, not like Christmas. Since this place is mine to do with what I want, I figured I was going to make it as Christmassy as I could. Usually, I argue with Gram and Caroline and Andrew and anyone else who happens to be by about how much is too much. And in my opinion, there's no such thing."

Emily grinned. "As long as you're not one of those crazies who has it looking like Christmas all year."

"You never know. I just might. Look at how beautiful it is in here." She gestured around the room, proud of what she'd done with all the odds and ends she'd found in storage at Gram's.

As Allie placed the packages under the tree, another knock sounded at the door. She opened it to find a disheveled Andrew standing there.

"Shouldn't you still be celebrating your wedding night? Or at least recovering from it? I know it's Christmas, but it's barely six AM."

Her tone was light, until she saw the expression on his face.

"What happened? Is Gram okay?"

"Gram's fine. No one's hurt, but something terrible has happened. You need to come with me right away."

Even though he assured her everyone was fine, dread filled her.

"Please tell me what's going on."

He came inside and grabbed her coat from the hook. He tossed it at her. "Put this on. And your boots."

Something inside her stomach knotted in a most painful way. If he wouldn't tell her, it had to be really bad.

"I need to know."

Andrew shook his head. "Please don't make me tell you. I can't."

Emily came in from the kitchen. "Does it have something to do with all the fire trucks I saw passing me on the way here?"

"It's the farm, isn't it?"

As he shook his head again, tears streamed down his face. "Not the farm. The barn and your greenhouse."

Now she knew why he couldn't tell her. She ran to his arms, and he held her while they both sobbed. The lavender business might have been hers, but he'd helped her build it. Every nail, every screw, every piece of wood, every piece of glass. Andrew's hands had touched them.

Layla entered the house. "We need to go. See what else we can do. They've got fire crews from the surrounding area coming, and we should be there to direct things."

As she pulled away from her brother, she looked at her new sister-in-law. "I didn't just ruin your wedding. I ruined your wedding night."

"No. Things like this happen to people all the time. My

wedding was wonderful, and while my wedding night is none of your business, I will say I have no complaints. So, let's get you all bundled up, and we'll go see what we can do to support the emergency workers."

Allie looked over Emily. "But your kids…"

"I took the liberty of calling my cousin, Veronica Quintana. She's good with kids, and she'll stay here to look after them for now. Once we figure out a plan, I'll let you know," Layla said.

Emily nodded. "Veronica has watched them before. It'll be all right." Then she hesitated. "But it's Christmas. Surely she would rather-"

"Help a family in need. It's what we do. She'll be here soon, then you can get back to the hospital."

The firm way Layla addressed Emily made Allie grateful her brother had chosen such a level-headed woman. Right now, she couldn't think, let alone make responsible decisions about someone else's children.

"Thank you," Emily said. "I can't believe you would go to so much trouble with everything your family has going on."

Layla smiled. "Allie speaks very fondly of you, and given that she was so determined to help you, we're determined to help you. It will all work out."

As Andrew helped her with her coat, she shoved her feet into her snow boots. There wasn't much snow, but enough that it was cold, and her feet would appreciate the extra warmth.

They hadn't gone far before she could see the blaze in the distance. She thought about the email she had just treasured about her products and how her plans had so easily come to ruin.

Fire trucks blocked the driveway, so they parked in the

grass, or at least where the grass would be if it wasn't covered with snow.

Watching her barn and greenhouse burn, she felt the tears being sucked from her face. But even that moisture wasn't enough to stop it.

"You have to stand back," a fireman said. "We don't want anyone getting too close to the fire."

Another truck arrived on the scene. So many firetrucks. So much fire. The men jumped out, but instead of going to work on the barn, they started doing things to the house.

"What's going on? Why aren't you trying to put out the barn and the greenhouse?" She stepped in front of one of the firemen, hoping he could make it make sense.

"We can't save them. Our only hope is to keep it from spreading to the house and any of the other buildings. Now please, we need you to get back."

He gestured to a corner of the yard, where Gram stood, huddled with Caroline. Her parents stood nearby, looking irritated that they'd been pulled from their beds so early. Allie ran to Gram.

"I'm so sorry," Gram said, putting her arms around her.

Caroline moved around, to hold Allie from the other side. "Hayden is with the other firefighters, doing what he can. He said that as the various volunteers in the area heard that it was Bigby Farm, they all came."

They might have all come, but it wasn't enough to save Allie's dream.

"We were making them coffee and tea, but then they said the fire was too close to the house, and we all had to get out." Gram looked irritated at having her plans thwarted, but as the wind shifted and embers flew in their direction, she was glad that they had chosen to keep her family safe.

That had to be the only bright side of the whole situation. That everyone was safe.

"How did this happen?" she asked, looking around. Andrew had gone over to talk with one of the firefighters, and Layla was examining another. From the looks of things, the one firefighter had some kind of injury.

"Andrew says he looked out the window of his tiny house and saw a strange light. When he went outside to get a better look, that's when he discovered the fire. He called 911 right away, then us, then Gram, and while he was doing that, he drove over to get you." Caroline looked sorrowful as she explained what had happened.

"But how did the fire start?" Allie asked, looking around again.

Caroline gave her another squeeze. "We don't know. They'll have to do an investigation, and we may not know for some time. What matters is that we're all okay, and we all have each other."

Another truck pulled up, and more men jumped out. Though it was just a plain pickup truck, all the men had fire gear, and Allie had to admit that it did make her feel good to know so many people were coming out to help.

One of the men drew nearer. Cole.

"James lent me his gear so I could come and see if there was anything I could do. I'm technically not signed up with the Arcadia Valley volunteer fire department, but I do have training from the military in handling emergencies like this." He shifted nervously, like he wasn't sure of his welcome.

"But before I volunteer my services to them, I have to let you know that if there is anything I can do to help you, please ask. We talked about how in the past, I just did things for you without knowing if that's what you really wanted.

So, I'm asking you. I know you don't know what you need right now, and you may not know for a long time, but if there is anything you need, I am here."

She hadn't expected to be so moved by his words. Not when she used to dread everything that came out of his mouth. But there was a sincerity in him that made her feel safe. Over the past day, Cole had been there for her. He'd defended her, he'd driven her to the hospital. And, he'd taken care of a stranger's children when no one else was there to do so. He was a good man. And she had underestimated him.

"Thank you," she said, knowing it wasn't adequate in expressing how she felt. But right now, as she watched everything she'd ever worked for go up in smoke, she wasn't sure she was capable of expressing anything at all.

He gave a nod, then jogged over to where some of the firefighters had gathered, presumably to discuss their next move.

For a few minutes, she just stood there, noticing the sick way the flames consumed her business. At least it was the old barn. The new barn, where the Bigbys held the summer camp and rented the space for events, stood in the distance, guarded by firefighters, ready to prevent sparks from spreading. How many thousands of plans had been destroyed? How many tins of salve, waiting to be shipped? Even her computer, which held the records of all the people who had ordered from her, was in that barn.

She'd have to issue refunds, of course, but she wasn't even sure she'd know how to figure out who to send money to. All of it, gone.

Someone came up to them and said something to Gram. Gram tugged at Allie and turned her in the other direction. Some women had set up a small canopy near the street for them to use to get some protection from the weather. It was kind of them, but what was a little snow when your entire life was burning down? Literally burning down.

Allie's mother stood at the edge of the tent, looking at her with the same superior judgmental expression she always used when it came to Allie. She stared back at her.

"I hope you're happy," Allie said, looking her in the eye. "I am one hundred percent the failure you've always said I am. I lost my job, my car, and now my business. I have literally nothing left to lose except my life. But you probably won't be satisfied until that happens too."

She didn't wait for a response as she walked on by. Admitting the truth out loud had always been too painful for her. But now, having said the words, it felt good to express the thing she most feared. That her mother's rejection of her was on that deep a level.

But when someone directed her to a chair and she sat, able to once again look upon the destruction, she felt an odd sense of peace. She had literally lost everything. However, the warmth of Gram's hand in hers and the gentle touch of Caroline's arm around her shoulders told her that she still had all the things that were important to her.

"We're going to get through this," Caroline said. "I heard what Cole said to you. And you have to know that goes a thousand times for all of us."

Though she had briefly sobbed in her brother's arms when she'd first learned the news, her tears since then had barely stung the backs of her eyes. But now, as she sat among her loved ones, helpless to do anything about the horrific events unfolding, she began to sob. A gut-wrenching, heartbreaking sob that should have indicated the depth of her pain, but didn't even come close.

## 12

Allie had lost everything. As Cole walked through the charred remains of what had been her barn and greenhouse, he could find nothing worth saving. They'd managed to prevent the fire from spreading to any of the other buildings on Bigby Farm, but the blaze had been too hot to stop it from destroying everything she owned.

Cole understood the pain of losing everything you ever dreamed of. That's how he'd felt when the Army doctor told him he couldn't recommend a return to active duty. And yet, he could not adequately express that in a way he thought would be helpful to her.

The crunch of boots sounded behind him. He turned to see Allie. "I don't know what to say," he said.

"Then please don't say anything. I'm tired of platitudes and the vague, 'I'm sorrys'. People mean well, and I don't want to take away from their desire to comfort me. You said you would do anything for me, so could you please just leave it? Don't try to make me feel better. I want to be sad right now. I need to be sad right now. So, will you just let me?"

She started to cry, and he wanted to hug her, but was afraid.

"I understand. When I had my accident, people kept saying things they thought were encouraging, and I just wanted them to shut up. My life was over, and nothing they said would change that. So you do what's best for you. And I'm here to let you."

She stopped crying and looked up at him. "Tell me about what happened. All I know is you were injured, and then you had to leave the Army. You know my tragedy, I want to know yours."

The funny thing about coming back to Arcadia Valley was that no one had asked him about his accident. Everyone in the Army wanted to know every gory detail, but here, they just knew there was one, and that seemed to be enough.

"Not much to tell. We were on a routine training mission, and one of the new guys didn't follow directions on a jump. I had already jumped, and he got nervous and didn't wait for the signal. He hit me in the back, boots first. Our chutes got tangled, and when we landed, he was on top of me. Broke my back in three different places. The doctors say I'm lucky to be able to walk, and I'm grateful. But it took several surgeries, and I can no longer handle the physical demands of my job."

It was amazing how easy it was to tell Allie about what had happened. Just the bare details, but it felt good to get them out.

"You really loved being in the Army, didn't you?"

The knowing look she gave him made Cole feel a little

less alone in the situation. Most of his Army friends, especially the lifers like him, always fell into an awkward silence when his accident came up. Especially now once he'd been discharged.

"It was all I wanted to do with my life."

Allie looked thoughtful, and she nodded slowly. "I can't imagine what that would be like. I've wanted to do so many different things. Until my lavender business, I couldn't ever commit to anything long-term. I suppose I wasn't even really committed to that, considering I still had a job. And now-"

A long sigh escaped her as she looked around at the damage. "Is it worth it to start over? The insurance will cover the buildings, and I suppose some of my supplies. But it doesn't cover the fact that I'll have to make everything again, and that I'll have to wait for the new harvest to get more lavender."

The hopelessness on her face was something Cole thought only he knew. But for some reason, the fact that the usually positive woman sounded so discouraged made it not okay.

She gave another long sigh. "Maybe this is a sign that I shouldn't have even tried. Maybe I'm the loser my parents have always said I am. But since I can't even keep a job at the local Gas N' Shop, what else is there for me?"

"You're not a loser."

The words came out with more force than he had intended, because her eyes widened, and she took a step back. But maybe that was okay. How could Allie think that of herself, when she was smart, talented, and more creative than anyone else he knew?

"I'd like to think that, but I have to wonder if this is a sign from God that I'm headed in the wrong direction. If I was doing everything right, why would my barn burn down?"

"Where in the Bible does God promise it will be easy? The road is hard, and only the most determined will finish the race. Are you running to win, or are you just trying to survive?"

Though his words to Allie were supposed to be about her, he realized he was also speaking to himself. Since his accident, he had just been trying to survive. But he couldn't help thinking about the passage in First Corinthians that says in a race all the runners run, but only one gets the prize, and that people should run to get the prize. He had not been trying to get the prize. In fact, he had lost sight it completely.

In all of this, he'd been going about his business willy-nilly, pouting over the fact that he couldn't do the job he wanted to do. But had he given any thought to what God wanted him to do?

He turned his attention back to Allie. "It's funny how we're in the same situation. And I was just thinking how, in all this time that I've been upset about everything that happened to me, I haven't once stopped to ask God about the direction I should take. I've asked Him why this happened, but I never thought to ask, 'What's next?'"

He examined Allie's face for any sign that she understood. For a moment, it looked like she was going to reject his advice. But then she nodded slowly.

"Gram and I have been talking about things like that a lot lately. You know, praying and talking to God. Asking God for help to do the things we know we're supposed to do, but can't."

Wow. One more thing he hadn't fully considered. Silly if he thought about it, except that most people didn't often give a lot of thought to prayer. Prayer seemed to be the afterthought, the last resort. What would his life look like, if he'd taken the time to pray first? What would everyone's lives look like?

"I think we're on the same journey," he said, hoping she wouldn't take his words as one more inappropriate move on his part. Would she see him as trying to help?

She looked at him suspiciously, then shrugged. "Maybe."

"I've pushed too far, haven't I? I hope you know that I'm just here as a friend. I'm not looking for anything more. I realized that you were right about a lot of things. I've been selfish in my pursuit of you. I never asked what you wanted, and you made it clear that what you want is to be left alone. So, I'm choosing to respect that, and I apologize if I over-stepped."

Allie's cousin Caroline approached. "Come on, Allie. There's nothing we can do here. It's cold, and you'll catch your death. I know it feels like your world is ended, but I promise you, the sun will come up again tomorrow. So, let's keep you healthy to enjoy it. The ladies brought over some food, including those muffins you like so much from the Slice of Heaven Bakery. I know you keep saying you're not hungry, but you have to eat."

Cole watched as Caroline hugged her, and she hugged her back. Maybe he wasn't quite over her yet, because he was surprised by the longing he felt at watching that simple embrace. It would have been nice to have been able to hug her, not in a creepy way, but just to offer comfort, especially because they did share the connection of their broken dreams.

Allie turned and gave him a soft smile. "Thank you for your encouraging words. I'll definitely think about them, and for sure, I'll spend more time in prayer over the direction God wants me to take now."

"You're welcome," he said. "This conversation helped me as much as it helped you. I, too, need to spend more time in prayer. Let me know if there's anything specific I can pray for you about. And if you decide to rebuild, I'd be honored to help."

She rewarded him with a smile. Funny how he hadn't realized until now how seldom that expression had been directed at him. And he would have to say that he really liked them, because, with that smile, Allie Bigby truly was the most beautiful woman in the world. A man would do just about anything to have those looks shining in his direction.

"It's too soon to say what will happen, but I appreciate the offer."

Caroline turned and stared at her cousin. "What do you mean, it's too soon to say what will happen? Of course, you'll rebuild. What else would you do?"

A thoughtful expression crossed Allie's face, making her look ancient in spirit. "It depends on what God tells me to do. My life's a mess right now, and nothing makes sense. So maybe it's time I stopped doing whatever I want, and figure what God wants."

Did she understand how wise she sounded with those words? It was too bad all the people who made her think she was a loser couldn't hear them.

Caroline gave her another hug. "I completely understand. When Hayden and I were dealing with wedding crazies, I felt like I was losing my mind trying to please everyone by putting on the wedding of the century. I hadn't asked God at all what He thought. And then one day, Hayden and I were in Twin Falls having lunch on what felt like a rare occasion where we could be alone and just enjoy each other's company. For some reason, I cried out to God, and I asked Him what the point of all this insanity was. I realized that the thing that mattered most was being with Hayden."

A contented smile filled Caroline's face. "I told him that, and he felt the same way. We were both so over planning the wedding and just wanted to get on with being together. So, we walked to the courthouse and got married. Mom says someday we will regret not having a big wedding. But that was never important to us. What was important was each other. Taking a moment to stop and ask God helped me refocus my priorities. I pray that you'll have the same clarity about your future."

He'd heard something similar from Andrew in the emergency room when he talked about his wedding. The getting married was the only thing that mattered, not where it was or any of the other fancy details. Andrew had even said the same thing when it came to the music. Not that either Allie or Cole were getting married anytime soon, but he supposed that same level of clarity applied to every area of life. They got so busy getting stressed out over details that they missed the big picture.

"Well, I'll tell you one thing," Allie said. "All of this ridiculousness has taught me that there is no way I'm having a big fuss over my wedding. I'll probably do what you just did, except we won't have even started planning the event. I'll just grab the guy, and we'll go get hitched somewhere."

Caroline laughed. "You're not giving him a choice in the matter?"

"If it's meant to be, then he'll be just fine with it."

Funny, in all of his imaginings about marrying Allie, he'd always pictured them in his uncle's church, surrounded by friends and family. One more reason they probably weren't as compatible as he'd thought. For as much time as he'd spent thinking about Allie and what he hoped for in their future, he clearly hadn't considered what she wanted.

"Just keep the door open to the possibility that God might have something different in mind for you," Caroline said, grinning. "In case you haven't figured it out, God's plans can lead us to some strange places sometimes."

Once more, even though Caroline was speaking to her cousin, her words spoke directly to his soul. He certainly had gone on a very strange journey, one whose destination he didn't quite know yet.

Then Caroline turned to him. "I'll bet you never thought you'd be singing at Andrew's wedding or leading worship at church. I mean, you're good and all, but when you led worship in high school, I always got the impression that you wanted to be somewhere else. Even the past couple Sundays, it hasn't seemed like you really wanted to be there."

Busted. And that wasn't her giving him a hard time, that was God picking him up and shaking him to make him see the truth. Maybe, even though he wouldn't let Uncle Vince say it, God had brought him here to take Agnes's place when the church needed him the most. And maybe, instead of fighting it and being bitter, he just needed to accept that this was where God had him and to let God use him in this place.

"Thanks," he said. "I hate to admit it, but you're right. I've done the church a grave disservice by not giving you guys my all, by not giving God my all. I've been angry about my circumstances, and I need to let go of my will, and let God take over."

Caroline gave him a strange look. "Well I didn't mean it

that way, but if that's how you need to take it, good for you. Just so you know, I didn't intend it as an insult."

"I know you didn't. But it reflects what Allie and I were just talking about, seeking God's will. It's amazing how readily we take charge of our own lives, and miss what God's doing."

No wonder God hadn't shown up in all of his struggles recently. He probably had, but he had been too focused on himself to notice.

Allie had gone quiet again, continuing to stare at the rubble. The wind picked up, and blew something in her direction. he couldn't see what it was, but she had managed to grab it. Whatever the object was, it seemed to take all of her attention. Then she turned.

Tears were streaming down her face as she held up the object. It looked like some kind of plant or something.

"A fresh sprig of lavender," she said. "Completely unharmed by the fire. It had to have come from my greenhouse. I had a batch almost ready to harvest."

Caroline reached over and took her hand. "Maybe there is more left."

Given the amount of rubble, finding more would be impossible. It was a small miracle to even have this one piece. Allie gestured in the direction of the greenhouse.

"Not likely. The roof is caved in in most parts, and even in that corner, where it looks like the structure might still be intact, it's too dangerous to take a look. The firefighters have already warned me. It won't be cool enough for days, even with the snow. And by then, any remaining plants will be dead."

The despondent look she'd worn earlier seemed to have disappeared. Instead, her face was full of hope. Like such bad news didn't affect her anymore.

"I still think it's too early to decide to give up," Caroline said.

A new determination filled Allie's face. "Who said anything about giving up? It's too early to tell. The insurance adjuster won't be out until tomorrow. I don't know yet what I will have to work with. So, we'll see. But I have hope."

Of anything she could have said, this gave him the greatest feeling of joy. The desire to wait and see without making any rash decisions.

"Then let's get you inside and have some of those muffins before they're all gone," Caroline said. "You too, Cole."

He didn't know why Caroline's words were so unexpected, after all, he had known her for years. But it felt good in a strange way to have her be so welcoming.

"Yes," Allie said. "You should. I know you were here, helping with the fire, and Gram will be unhappy if we don't make sure everyone gets refreshment. Plus, as Andrew's friend, you might be able to convince him that we have everything in hand and he should go enjoy his honeymoon with his new wife."

If he hadn't already been given hope that things would work out, this gesture sealed it. She recognized what he'd done without him having to jump up and down to get her to pay attention to it. Maybe that had been his trouble all along. He'd do something nice for her and then bug her about it until she'd acknowledged him. People had told him over the years that love was about doing things for people without requiring recognition. But he'd wanted so badly to get her attention that he hadn't listened.

More importantly, she recognized his friendship with Andrew and saw him as a positive influence in her brother's life. One more thing he would have never expected from her.

He remembered from his parents' funeral services, Uncle Vince had encouraged him to look for the gift in tragedy. He hadn't been able to see it in any of his own tragedies, but at least, in the recent events involving Allie and him, she was starting to stop viewing him as the enemy.

# 13

---

Though everyone seemed to consider Allie the most upbeat person they knew, she was starting to think of positive thinking as being for the birds. Her insurance agent had told her that her loss wasn't covered because she hadn't paid her premium.

What a bunch of malarkey.

Granted, she was rather absent-minded about paying some of her bills. Okay, all of her bills. But as she looked through her checkbook, she could clearly see, plain as day, that she had just written her premium check. Some people might think that having carbon copies of your checks was old-fashioned. But Allie, knowing that she forgot things, liked being able to go back and look at the records.

She'd considered it a small miracle that her checkbook had even survived the fire. But she'd taken it out of her office only the night before Andrew's wedding to see how bad things really were for her financially. Only she'd run out of time in all the craziness. Which didn't matter. The only thing that mattered was that she had her checkbook, and she could clearly see where she had paid her insurance premium on December 1.

She drove back to Gram's, feeling a little more positive because at least this was, as she had hoped, just a misunderstanding. Maybe the insurance company had simply forgotten to notate in their records or notated it on the wrong record.

When she arrived, she tried not to groan when she realized that her parents were in the kitchen, and no one was there to run interference. Since the big bust-up at Andrew's wedding, Caroline and Gram had made sure that she wasn't alone with them. And every time either one of them opened their mouth to speak, either Caroline or Gram would shut down the conversation.

"Allison," her mother said, giving her the look that always spelled a lecture. "It's good you're here, so we can talk."

She looked around, hoping someone would come save her soon. "There isn't much to talk about. I have things I need to do."

Her father gave her a sharp glare. "Is that any way to talk your mother?"

She fought the urge to groan.

"I'm sorry. In case you hadn't noticed, I'm in the middle of a great personal tragedy, and I need to talk to the insurance adjuster before he leaves. If you don't mind, can we continue this discussion later?"

She thought that, all things considered, she was being quite grown up in her answer, especially because they still continued to have the expression that she was a being naughty child, and she hadn't done anything wrong.

The stern expression didn't leave her father's face. "You

keep avoiding us. Now that the wedding is over, we would like to get back to our lives."

Could that possibly mean that her parents were finally going to go home and get out of her hair? Allie was surprised they'd stayed this long, since her father still had to work. But somehow he'd found a way to make a telecommuting arrangement with his job.

Now, she just wished he'd go home.

"When are you planning on going back to Seattle?" She asked, trying to sound blasé about the whole thing.

Her father looked over at her mother. "We were thinking after the new year, which was our original plan. But with your life in shambles, our plans are in the air."

Shambles. An accurate description, but it felt extremely unfair, given his tone of voice.

"I'll be all right. I've had a lot of good conversations with Gram. We've been praying a lot, and I'm really overwhelmed by all the goodwill from the community. You don't have to worry about me."

As always, her answer wasn't good enough for her mother, who gave an exaggerated, disapproving groan.

"You put too much stock in an old fool and superstitious nonsense. It's time you grew up, got a real job, and built a real life for yourself."

Which insult was she supposed to respond to first? She was trying not to do her usual thing and snap at her mother. Lately, as she'd been praying about the situation with her parents, her mind kept going back to Proverbs, and how it said that a soft answer turns away wrath, but a sharp answer leads to strife. There had been a lot of sharp answers between her and her mother over the years, but she still hadn't figured out how to give a soft answer and still defend herself.

But did it matter? It seemed like regardless of what she said, her parents still believed the worst of her.

"I know you're worried about me, but I'll be fine. I've been fine thus far, and I know everything will work out okay."

Rage filled her mother's face. "Fine? From where I'm standing, everything in your life is a mess. The biggest mistake we ever made was letting you to stay here with Bart's mother. Maybe if we'd made you guys come with us, you wouldn't have bought in to Enid's ridiculous ideas, and you would be a stable, successful adult."

And had she gone with her parents, she would have continued feeling stifled and alone. She'd spent her entire life feeling like she wasn't good enough, especially when it came to her mother. She couldn't be the person her mother wanted her to, which was why she'd gotten along so well with her cousin Caroline. Caroline had felt the same way about her mother, and yet somehow, after all the years of fighting, the women had found a way to make amends.

True, Caroline's mother wasn't pleased with her over the whole elopement thing, but she hadn't been as harsh as she would have been in the past.

Could Allie and her mother find that same peace?

"I'm sorry you see it as a regret. I'm glad I got to stay here, because I find the city stifling. I know you don't agree with how I've been living my life, but you need to know that I'm happy."

Until she'd said the words out loud, she hadn't realized how true they were. She was happy. Yes, things got stressful at times, but overall, she was happy. Though most people didn't see working at the Gas N' Shop as a real job, Allie had enjoyed it. It gave her the chance to see her neighbors and catch up on everyone's news. She liked having her lavender business. Not the business part, but she enjoyed growing the plants, making products, and being at the farmer's markets, where she could talk to people and let them know how to improve their overall health.

Her parents might see that as a waste. But to her, it was a good life.

She looked at her mother. "Just what do you think makes a successful adult?"

She made an irritated noise. "A good job, for one."

"And what makes a good job?"

Once again, she looked at her like she was an idiot. "A decent salary to live on, good benefits, upward mobility, the usual things people look for in a career."

Not once had she mentioned what Allie thought was the most important thing. "What about happiness? Satisfaction?" She turned to her father. "Do you like your job? Are you happy with what you do?"

"What a ridiculous question," her mother said, not giving him the chance to answer.

"It should be a simple one," Allie said. "You spend most of your waking hours at work, so if you don't enjoy it, why do you do it?"

She kept her attention on her father, who looked thoughtful. "This sounds a lot like some of the conversations I've been having with Andrew. But to answer your question, yes, I do enjoy my job. It also happens to pay well and have good benefits. There's no sin in making good money."

"I never said there was. I just wish you guys could respect my choices and understand that this is my life. I'm not trying to be difficult, I'm just trying to live a good life and be happy."

The door opened and Gram walked in with the insurance adjuster, saving her from what was likely going to be an unsympathetic response from her parents.

"Allie," Gram said. "You're back. Did you find the receipt, showing that you paid your premium?"

She pulled out her checkbook. "No, because all of my receipts were in the office, which was in the barn that burned down. However, I do have the carbons of my checks, and as you can see, I wrote it on December first. That should have me paid up for the next six months."

The insurance adjuster shook his head. "I need a canceled check. This does me no good."

Her father stepped forward. "Bart Bigby. And you are?"

"Harold Faulkner. I work for Idaho Farm Insurance, and while I did come out to look at the damage, as I've explained to these ladies, the business policy Allie had has lapsed due to nonpayment."

Great. One more reason her parents would think she was irresponsible.

"I'm sure there must be a misunderstanding," her father said smoothly. "Isn't there a grace period? If she were to write you a new check right now, could we work something out?"

She hadn't been prepared for her father to stand up for her like that.

Faulkner, one more thing she could be glad of for her father's involvement, since she'd been too distraught to remember the man's name, coughed. "Well, under ordinary circumstances, there is a thirty day grace period. But this is not an ordinary situation. Technically, the policy has lapsed, and I'm not sure we can get it reinstated to pay on your daughter's claim."

Her father gave Faulkner a warm smile. She couldn't

remember the last time such a look had been directed at her.

"I understand. But surely there's a supervisor or someone we can talk to. In the meantime, when the bank opens, we'll see what we can find out about the payment gone astray. What can we work out?"

She could see how he did very well in business. So why didn't he use such diplomacy when dealing with his children? He obviously knew the power of the proverb she had been praying over lately, at least in trying to get his way with others. Could she find a way to use this side of him that she'd never seen before to bridge the gap between her and her parents?

"Well," Faulkner said. "It is the holidays, and I know how things sometimes can get lost in the mail. I'll talk to my supervisor. You check with the bank, and let's talk next week to see what we can figure out."

Tears sprang to her eyes. It wasn't a yes, but it wasn't the harsh denial she'd been getting used to. "Thank you so much. You don't know what this means to me."

At this point, though she was thanking Faulkner, what she wanted to do was run to her father and give him a big hug. Maybe he wasn't jumping up and down and supporting her in pursuing her dreams, but he was trying to help.

"I can't promise you anything," Faulkner said. "But I'll try. I live a couple towns over, in Kerrville, but we've heard of Bigby Farm. I believe my wife has brought the kids here for the Harvest Festival a time or two. Actually, I remember coming here as a boy for summer camp. It would be a shame to lose such a valuable part of our community history."

"Well," Gram said, putting her hands on her hips. "You and your family are welcome here anytime. And that's not a bribe. I don't think you can get in trouble for bribing insurance men, but if you can, I want you to know that I'm not bribing you. I welcome everyone here. Friends, family, enemies, and even the family we don't want."

Faulkner chuckled, but Allie noticed her mom looking uncomfortable. Her dad didn't look too pleased with the statement, either. But that was Gram's way. And if you didn't like the truth, you probably shouldn't come around. Which was probably why her parents didn't.

As Gram led Faulkner out, chattering about how the farm had changed since he'd come as a boy, Allie turned to her father.

"Thank you for what you said. I know nothing about this sort of thing, and it was helpful to have you presenting us with some options. It really means a lot to me."

Her family had never been much into hugging, but she stepped forward, following her earlier instinct to give her dad a hug.

For a moment, it felt awkward, and he was stiff. But then his posture loosened, and he hugged her back.

When she pulled away, he smiled at her. "You just have to know their game, that's all. They make money by collecting premiums and hoping they won't have to pay claims. Most insurance companies will find whatever excuse they can to deny a claim. This was just an attempt at denial number one. They'll probably try again, but we'll find a way to beat them."

It seemed almost like he had done an about-face. "I didn't think you supported my business," she said.

"I don't want to see my daughter being taken advantage of."

At least he hadn't fully contradicted her. But it would've been nice for him to say something a little more supportive.

She looked over at her mother, who hadn't said anything during the exchange. From the expression on her face, she wasn't sure she dared speak to her at this point. Why did her mother hate her so much?

"Now," he said. "We need to figure out what happened to that check. Does your bank store the image of canceled checks online for you?"

She looked at him blankly. What did that even mean? "I have no idea. I've never had a problem with missing checks before."

Her mother made a noise like she didn't believe her, and she wasn't about to tell her that the reason was because Andrew always helped with those things. For personal items, she always used cash that she kept in envelopes, sorted out for each budgeted purpose. But for business, Andrew helped her keep her books. At least until the past couple of months, when he'd gotten too busy with school and his wedding.

Not that Allie was blaming Andrew. She had assured him that she would be fine. But she'd been wrong.

"Do you have online access to your account?" Her dad asked. "I'm happy to take a look."

On one hand, she didn't want him to do so. Because then he would know just how little money she had. On the other hand, this was the first civil conversation they'd had, and she couldn't find it in her heart to tell him no, even though it would leave them with a worse impression of her.

She grabbed her laptop out of her bag and set it on the counter. She quickly logged in to her account, and surprised by what she saw.

"This isn't right," she said.

Her dad came around and looked over her shoulder. "What's not right?"

She scanned the account information. "There's too much money in here."

Her mother made a noise, like she couldn't comprehend those words coming out of her mouth.

"I should have about $200 in here," Allie said. "This is too much."

As she clicked on the account details section, she noticed a huge gap in the listing of cleared checks. She reached over and grabbed her checkbook. Glancing through the checks, she felt sick.

"All these bills that I paid, none of the checks have cleared. I don't understand what happened."

Though she was quick to note that her insurance check was indeed one of the ones that had not yet cleared, she saw another one that made her want to cry. Her heating bill. Actually, it was for the whole farm, but since she used most of it for her greenhouse, she paid it. The day of her accident, she'd been on her way to pay it in person and then drop all her bills off at the post office to mail.

She'd never gone to the post office.

She rummaged through her bag, trying to find the bills she was supposed to have mailed. They weren't there.

"What are you looking for?" her father asked, concern lining his face.

She couldn't admit what she'd done. Or not done, as the case might be. But it still didn't explain where her bills were.

Before she could answer, Gram reentered with Wade. "Look who came by," she said. "And just in the nick of time."

"It was nothing. Always glad to help a neighbor," Wade said.

She was almost afraid to ask, with everything else that had gone on. "What now?"

"Someone from the gas company was here to shut off the

gas and electric," Gram said. "He said we hadn't paid our bill. But I told him that we always pay our bill. And I know you said you were going to go do that. But he didn't want to listen to me. Fortunately, Wade was here, and he gave the man some money and he left."

She'd hoped that she could have privately had her revelation and made everything right. Unfortunately, that didn't seem to be how her life worked.

"I just realized something terrible," she said. "I'd been on my way to pay that bill and mail the others when I was in my accident. I was just looking through my purse to see where they were, but they're not here. I don't know what happened to all the bills I was supposed to pay that day."

"Well isn't that just typical," her mom said, making her feel like the little girl who was always in trouble.

"Could they still be in the car?" Gram asked, ignoring her.

Allie shook her head. "No. The insurance company came and got my car the other day since it was totaled. I took everything out. If the bills had been in there, I would have noticed."

"Maybe you threw them away," her mom said. "You probably weren't paying attention, just like always, and accidentally tossed them. You never pay attention. That's what has gotten you into all these messes, and once again everyone else is bailing you out. When are you going to learn?"

The worst part of what she was saying was that it was all true. How was she ever supposed to learn how to be a responsible adult, like everyone wanted of her, when she couldn't even keep track of a few simple envelopes?

"Mary." Allie's father's voice came out like one of the warnings he always gave his daughter.

"No. I am not going to let you or anyone else defend her this time. Allison deserves every bad thing that has happened to her because when you come right down to it, it's all her fault."

The nastiness in her voice made Allie want to run and hide, the way she always did. But she knew there was a kernel of truth in those words. She often got distracted, and being distracted caused a lot of problems for her.

"I'm sure that fire in her greenhouse started because she left something on and forgot about it, and it's going to be one more reason why she needs to learn to grow up. Except everyone keeps defending her and making excuses for her, and she never learns. She's been this way since she was a child. I kept hoping that she would grow up to be responsible, but no one has let her do that."

She wasn't even sure she could answer her mother's charges if she wanted to. Gram came and put her arm around Allie. "None of this is your fault. Your mother is just bitter that you're the reason people found out about her affair with Jim Johnson and your father lost his job, so he had to find something elsewhere."

Then Gram turned and stared at Allie's mother. "I still don't know why Bart took you back, with the way you were carrying on. But when you sleep with your husband's boss, you have to expect that there will be consequences. Blaming Allie and holding a grudge against her for it does no one any good. If you want her to learn to accept responsibility for her actions, then maybe you should take responsibility for yours."

She turned her gaze to her grandmother. "What are you talking about?"

Gram continued staring at Mary. "Now's your chance. Accept responsibility. Show your daughter how it's done."

Her father shook his head slowly. "I thought we moved beyond this. I forgave Mary, it's true. We went through counseling, and I believe as a result of the counseling, it made our marriage stronger."

"But how did it affect your children?" Gram asked. "You weren't there, Bart, but I will never forget walking in on Mary telling Allie that she was an irresponsible brat and that it was her fault the family was such a mess."

The memory washed over her. How could she have forgotten? All these years, she'd wondered why her mother hated her. But now she remembered. She'd forgotten her homework and had run back to the house to get it. When she walked into the house, she'd seen her mother on the couch, half-naked, in a very intimate embrace with Jim Johnson. Her mother had told her not to tell, but how could she not?

After that, her mother blamed her. If she hadn't been irresponsible and forgotten her homework, none of the bad things in the family would've happened. Her family wouldn't have had to move. While it had been a fight for them to agree to let Andrew stay and finish high school among his friends, her mother had never argued that Allie needed to come with them.

Tears filled her eyes as she realized that her mother's condemnation of Allie's irresponsibility was her way of not taking responsibility for her affair. Just like Gram had said.

She turned to her mother. "Mom, I'm sorry that I forgot my homework and walked in on you. And I'm sorry that I blurted out at the dinner table what I saw. You're right. I should have had more self-control. But you should have been able to control yourself too. And you shouldn't have blamed me all these years for everything that happened."

As she looked back at the domino effect of her catching

her mother in a bad situation, she realized she wasn't the one who started it. It was her mother's bad choice. And the bad choices of everyone as the events unfolded. Her dad shouldn't have punched his boss for sleeping with Allie's mom. Dad's boss shouldn't have done a lot of things in the situation, but he also didn't need to fire a man with a family on the spot. Her dad could've stayed in Arcadia Valley, but he'd been too humiliated to try harder to find a more local job. And yet, the jobs he'd gotten since were far better than anything he could've found had he stayed.

People's mistakes caused both good and bad things to happen, but it was their choice on how they handled it.

Cole's face flashed in Allie's mind. Allie was no better than her mother. True, he had done a lot of bad things to Allie. But she had also reacted inappropriately. And like her mother, Allie held grudges she shouldn't have held.

She gave her grandmother a squeeze. "Thank you for encouraging me to pray about my difficult situations lately. I just realized that we all make mistakes and do bad things to each other, sometimes on purpose, and sometimes by accident."

Cole had truly never meant any harm to her, she believed that now. Just like she knew she hadn't intended to ruin her family's lives with her actions.

"But it's our response to difficult situations that's important." She looked over at her father. "You say Mom's affair made your marriage stronger in the end. But you two have always treated me like the bad guy, because I supposedly started all the negative things that happened. If your marriage really is stronger, don't you think you should give me credit because I spoke up instead of keeping Mom's secret?"

Her dad nodded. "Until Mom said something, I guess I

didn't realize that's what was happening. You have to admit, your mother has been right about how irresponsible you are. I just never thought that it was because of the vendetta until now."

Allie hadn't either. But as she saw the fury on her mom's face, she knew. That's what all of this was about.

She turned to her mother. "You still have nothing to say?"

At her mother's stony silence, Allie realized it wasn't her problem. She had her own things to take responsibility for, but her mother's hatred of her was no longer one of them. However, as Allie moved forward, she's going to have to remember this lesson, especially as it pertained to Cole.

## 14

———

Though the old adage was that no news was good news, Cole hated having to wait for information on Allie's greenhouse and barn. Despite his friendship with the Bigbys, it still didn't feel right, driving over to see how things were going. They were all probably very busy, and he didn't want to risk bothering them, especially Allie.

But as he saw her new car parked at the Gas N' Shop, Cole couldn't help stopping. He could top off his tank, grab a cup of terrible coffee, and casually ask her how things were going. However, as he pulled into the parking lot, he wondered if that was a bad idea. How many times had he used the, "We just happened to be in the same place," excuse as a way to talk to her in the past? It hadn't gone over very well, and now, it seemed a little dishonest. Especially when he'd told her he was past all that.

But it didn't mean he couldn't go in and say hi, telling her the truth that he'd seen her car and was thinking about her.

When he entered the store, Allie was standing at the

counter, talking to the woman who'd been so horrible to her, Nadia.

"I just thought that if we can talk things out, maybe we can work past our differences," Allie was saying.

"As I told you," Nadia said in the nasty tone of voice Cole remembered, "this is a place of business. I don't have time for idle chitchat."

Allie didn't falter. "I would be happy to meet you when you're off, wherever you want. We could grab a burger at the diner, some margaritas at El Corazon, muffins at A Slice of Heaven Bakery, coffee at The Beanery, or we could even do something outside of town, so you don't have to be seen with me."

He had to give her credit for her creative ideas. She was doing everything possible to make this easy on Nadia.

"I'd like to enjoy my time off, thank you very much. And as you can see, we have a customer, so you need to leave and I need to get back to work." She sounded so hostile, and he felt bad for Allie, because she was clearly trying hard to do the right thing.

As much as Allie tried to say they were different people now, at the very core, she was still the person he had always admired. She cared about others, even hateful women like Nadia.

"Actually, I didn't need anything. I saw Allie's car and I wanted to stop to see how things were going with her greenhouse and barn." He kept his voice firm, especially since it seemed to intensify Nadia's glare.

She gave a snort. "So that's what this is about. With your side business out of commission, you're hoping that if you kiss up to me, you'll get your old job back. Well, I've got news for you, it's not going to happen. Ever."

The strength he saw rising in Allie was different from

what he'd seen in her before. She turned and smiled at him. "That's really sweet of you, thanks. We're doing the best we can, given the circumstances."

The look she gave him was another one of the rare genuine smiles Cole had been hoping to see more of. But it didn't last long, because she had returned her attention back to Nadia.

"As for getting my old job back, I realized that you probably did me a favor and gave me a wake-up call about what I really wanted from my life. I had to almost lose my lavender business, but I know now what's important to me, and where I need to focus my attention. A while back, Andrew challenged me, saying I feared success, so I never gave it a real shot. But I'm done with that, and I no longer need the security blanket of this job."

Was it wrong of him to want to tell her that he was proud of her? Maybe, but hopefully, he'd get a chance someday. Based on their conversation after the fire, he knew that this newfound determination had been the result of Allie wrestling with God to find her direction.

Nadia, however, didn't seem to be impressed. "Well, goody for you. If you don't mind, I'll skip attending the parade you seem so intent on throwing. Some of us have work to do."

"I don't want to throw a parade. But I do want to clear the air between us. I'd hoped that we could have a conversation, and get to know one another before the difficult part. But you are too blinded by your dislike of me to be willing to do so. Fine. We'll do it the hard way."

Allie straightened as she looked directly at her. "You're Jim Johnson's daughter, aren't you?"

"So what if I am?"

"I had a revelation the other day about why my mother hates me."

Nadia snorted again. "There's a big surprise. It figures that even your own mother couldn't love you."

He wanted to shake the nasty woman for her unkind comments. But Allie simply smiled.

"She thinks I ruined her life because I forgot my homework and walked in on her having an affair. With your dad."

He couldn't believe what she'd just said, yet the lack of surprise on Nadia's face told him that she had spoken the truth.

Allie leaned forward on the counter. "It ruined your life, too, didn't it?"

"My mom divorced my dad and made us move to Salt Lake City to be by her relatives. We had a good life here, and you destroyed it because you couldn't keep your mouth shut."

He was proud of Allie the way she didn't back off. She straightened, and calmly said, "No. Your dad did because he couldn't keep it in his pants. And my mom did because she couldn't either. It's easy to blame the messenger, but I didn't do anything wrong."

"I'm glad you were here for this," Allie said, turning to him. "I blamed you for a lot of bad things that happened in my life, some of which you did do. But some of it is really my fault for reacting inappropriately. You did not cause my car accident. I should have been paying more attention. Yes, I was distracted by thoughts of you, but that's my problem for being unable to control my frustration. I'm sorry for blaming you. And, when I get back on my feet, I'm going to pay you back for my deductible. It wasn't your responsibility to pay, but it was really kind of you to do so."

Before he could respond, she turned back to Nadia. "I

know that all of this nonsense between us has been about you punishing me for revealing our parents' affair. But they were in the wrong and nothing you do to me will ever change that. It's just going to keep you in misery. So, it's time for you to let go and move on. I forgive you for every nasty thing you've said about and done to me."

Nadia's face had turned bright red, so red, that he was sure it might explode.

"You don't know anything," she said.

"Maybe not. I've never been a very vindictive person. But I've lived with one most of my life. And I can tell you that until you find a way to deal with the emptiness in your heart, you're never going to feel better. I don't know why moving to Salt Lake City was so bad for you. But I hope, now that you're back here, you put the past behind you, and find a way to build a good life for yourself."

She didn't look like she appreciated Allie's words. "As I've been telling you, this is a place of business. You need to leave, or I'll call the police and have you arrested for trespassing."

Allie's shoulders rose and fell like she was disappointed by her response. "Fair enough. But if you do decide you want to talk, the door's always open. And, if I may be so bold, you're welcome to join us in Arcadia Valley Community Church anytime. Pastor Harris has given us a lot of good counsel, and I know he'd help you too."

Nadia made a noise. "So basically, you're just telling me that you think I'm crazy and need help. Yeah. Good plan for making peace."

The wounded look on Allie's face made him wish he could give her a hug. But just as quickly as it had appeared, a new expression replaced it. Compassion.

"No. I didn't mean it that way at all, I'm sorry," she said.

"I just meant that whenever any of us need someone to talk to, he's been a good listener. Maybe it would help you sort out your anger over what happened between our parents, then you could move on. I just think you're wasting a lot of energy on hating me when you could be doing something really good with your life. Obviously, Dan sees something in you and thinks highly of you. Imagine what you could accomplish if you had all your energy focused on that."

The door jangled open, and Allie turned back to him, looping her arm through his. "Come on. I was just headed over to your place to see how Jess is doing."

The anger hadn't left Nadia's face. He prayed that something in Allie's words would soften her heart. He couldn't imagine having gone through something like that. He vaguely remembered hearing something from Andrew about it, but it had never really impacted his friend.

They stepped out into the fresh air, and he was glad it had warmed up slightly. The snow was gone, the sun was out, and it looked like it was going to be a beautiful day.

The sincerity on her face as she looked at him once they got into the parking lot made him wish his pursuit of her hadn't completely ruined their chance at being friends.

"I meant what I said in there," Allie said. "I treated you unfairly and blamed you for a lot that wasn't your fault. I'm really sorry. I hope that moving forward, things will be different between us."

She held out her arms to him like she was offering him a hug. "Will you forgive me?"

Holy cow. Allie wanted to hug him. Now he knew that the transformation in her had come from God. He had clearly been working in her heart.

He stepped forward and into her arms. Though he could

have stayed there forever, breathing in her lavender scent, he gave her a quick embrace, then pulled away.

"Of course, I forgive you. I hope you can forgive me as well. I did a lot of boneheaded things over the years, and looking back, I didn't respect you as I should have. You told me to leave you alone multiple times, as did your brother and a number of our other friends, I didn't listen. That was wrong of me, and I'm sorry."

Something passed between them, a silent recognition of the growth they'd both undergone.

She smiled at him. "I forgive you too. I know it was awkward for you to have to witness what happened in there. But I'm glad you did, because the epiphany I had about Nadia's hatred of me happened at the same time I realized how unfair I've been to you."

The customer who'd been in the store walked out and looked at Allie. "I don't know what happened between you and Nadia in there, but if I were you, I'd steer clear of her for a while. I've never seen her this furious before. I'm sure it was a misunderstanding, but if I were you, I'd give it some time before clearing things up."

"Thanks, Kate." Allie turned and gestured at Cole. "Do you two know each other? Kate Groves, this is Cole Anderson. Kate is the manager of the Arcadia Valley Farmer's Market, and Cole is filling in for Agnes as the worship leader at Arcadia Valley Community Church."

Kate smiled at him and held out her hand. "It's a pleasure. We all miss her so much, but you did a wonderful job at the Christmas pageant."

Though her enthusiasm bolstered his spirits at filling such big shoes, he hated how she made it sound like Agnes's absence was only temporary. Though the information hadn't been made public yet, she had spoken to Uncle Vince the other day. Cole hadn't been privy to the entire conversation, but Uncle Vince had shared that she likely would not be returning.

Which meant the full-time job was his if he wanted it.

But even after his conversation with Allie, he was no closer to knowing God's will in that direction than he'd been before. Would this newfound understanding between them give him the opportunity to ask her how she'd found such clarity?

Unfortunately, this wasn't the time or place to figure that out. So, he smiled at Kate and said, "Thank you. Agnes has been my rock for so many years. It was weird, taking her place."

"Well, no offense to Agnes, but your style is a little fresher than hers, and I think a lot of the younger generation will relate to you better. I know we're not supposed to be focused on the person on stage, but sometimes Agnes was hard to follow because we were all so worried that she was going to keel over at any minute. She must be what, a hundred years old?"

She looked like she was trying to sound as respectful as possible, even though Agnes probably wouldn't have appreciated such a description.

Cole tried not to laugh. Hadn't that been his own impression of Agnes? "I believe she's in her 80s. I just hope it's not too much of a distraction having a new guy on stage."

"Not so much the new guy, but there may have been some women giggling at how cute he is." Kate nudged Allie. "But rumor has it that someone has already stolen his heart."

Great. Just great. They had just made peace over this very issue. How was it that even though he had done everything he possibly could to make things seem completely aboveboard, people were still gossiping about him and Allie?

Allie nudged Kate back. "Don't believe everything you hear. You know how the rumor mill works."

"Yeah, sorry." She looked over at him. "I hope you know I didn't mean anything by my comment. You won't have any matchmaking interference from me."

Then she returned her gaze to Allie. "Speaking of the rumor mill, I heard your complete production is a total loss. Is there anything I can do?"

"Unfortunately, that information is true. The good news is, I'm working with the insurance company and hopefully, we'll come to an agreement soon. Right now, the only thing there is for anyone to do is pray. So just pray that everything will be sorted out as quickly and efficiently as possible, and hopefully, we'll be back to normal soon."

She shook her head. "No. I don't want things to be back to normal. I've learned a lot through this trial, and I'd like to think I've grown as a result. I don't want to go back to where I was before the fire. I want to fully live out the person God has made me to be."

He loved the look Kate gave her. Like Kate, too, had also seen the growth in her and could appreciate the woman she'd become.

"That's a great prayer," she said. "Is it weird for me to tell you that I'm happy for you?"

Allie gave her a quick hug. "Not at all. In a strange way, it makes sense. Thanks for being willing to be there for me. I'll let you know if there's anything else you can do."

Movement inside the store caught Cole's eye. They all turned to see Nadia standing in the doorway, arms crossed in front of her, an angry expression on her face.

"We better get out of here," Allie said. "Nadia wasn't joking about calling the police. I've seen her do it before."

She gave Kate another quick hug. "I'll be in touch. In case you're worried about the farmers market, we're still committed to our usual space."

"I'm not worried at all. The most important thing is that you and your family are all okay." She turned and smiled at him. "And it was nice officially meeting you. I hope, even after Agnes comes back, you'll stay in some capacity. We really enjoy your music."

Allie gave him an approving look. "He is good, isn't he? Now that I don't hate him anymore, I can actually appreciate the fact that I like his worship music."

Now that was unexpected. As Kate walked to her car, he stared at Allie. "What do you mean by that?"

"Well since I'd sworn to hate you, I couldn't exactly like your music. Now that I've opened my mind to accepting that you aren't the world's most awful human being, I'm finding a lot more things to like about you. But seriously, we should go. I'll see you at your brother's place."

And just like that, she was in her car, heading for his brother's farm. How crazy that things seemed so normal between them. Like they were friends.

When they got there, she went straight inside. Neither Jess nor James had said anything to him about the baby news. Nor had they mentioned their thoughts on both Allie's and Cole's slips. As far as he knew, this was the first Allie had even been over.

James came out of his garage as he got out of his truck.

"Jess asked her to come over. She's been feeling bad about everything that happened, but knew it was more than a phone call. Especially with everything Allie has had going on. We both overreacted when you shared Jess's news. And I should've said something sooner, but I wasn't sure how to go about it. I'm sorry."

He shook his head. "It's all right. If it was my baby, I would've been mad to not be the first to know."

"From what Jess says, we might still not know if it hadn't been for Allie figuring it out."

"She said Jess was planning something special for you. I'm sorry I ruined it."

James smiled. "She was disappointed it wasn't a surprise, but she still did the thing she'd been planning. She had me open a big sister shirt she'd made for Caitlin. It was cute, and even though I knew about the baby, I appreciated the thought she put into it."

Then James nodded toward the house. "How are things with you and Allie? You haven't said much, other than when you got home from the hospital, that she wasn't contagious, and a brief description of what happened to her greenhouse and barn. Is it safe for us to go in there?"

He couldn't help laughing. Now that he and Allie had figured things out between them, he wasn't as offended by people's remarks. Actually, he wished he'd had the maturity sooner to see what had really been going on.

"Actually, we're good. Really good. I'm surprised at the connection we've developed. I'm almost tempted to say we might even be friends."

His brother patted him on the back as they headed toward the house. "Just make sure she says it first. The trouble you had with her before is that you read more into her kind actions than she intended."

Wise advice. Yes, Allie had asked for and given forgiveness for their past. She'd even hugged him. But she'd also hugged her friend Kate. Even though Cole had thought there might be a connection between the two of them, he'd definitely be mindful of guarding his heart and not presuming too much.

Still, when they entered the house, and Allie's laughter rang throughout, Cole couldn't help feeling a twinge that wished they could be something more. A woman like her, who was smart, beautiful, and had such a deep desire to follow God and do the right thing was a rare find indeed.

## 15

Sitting in Jess's kitchen, drinking tea, and laughing over the latest Caitlin story made her life seem not so difficult anymore. The baby was sleeping, which gave them a rare chance to catch up uninterrupted. Though she felt good about her attempt at making peace with Nadia, burying the hatchet with Cole, and even the fact that the rest of her world was mostly in ruins, this precious time was what Allie needed to make her life feel complete. Usually, she'd go into her greenhouse and inhale the loving scent of lavender.

But that wasn't possible anymore. However, she had almost a dozen plants in pots in Gram's window, and sitting here with Jess, she could see two more of her plants that she had potted for her friend as a gift. And, come spring, her field would bloom again.

All was not lost.

"You miss your plants, don't you?" Jess said. "I thought about steeping some of the lavender tea you made for me, but I didn't know if that would be too painful for you."

Allie looked up at her friend. "Not at all. I was just

thinking how happy it makes me to realize that even though my greenhouse plants are gone, their legacy lives on. You have some in your kitchen, and I think about the countless plants I sold at the Farmer's Market, and how many of them are living happily in someone's home. I still have my fields, which will come alive again in spring, and I can start a new greenhouse. So, make the tea, and we can dream about how wonderful it's going to be in the future."

It felt good to say out loud that she planned on rebuilding. At first, it had been a secret dream in her heart. But more and more, as she talked about it, it felt like the only direction she could go. More than that, it felt like the direction God wanted her to go.

"I'm glad. You know that I'll help you any way I can, well, at least as much as I can, given that I'm going to have my hands full with Caitlin and a new baby."

Allie looked over at Jess. "Yes, how did that go with James? I feel terrible for how it all came out. I want to make sure that forgive me."

"At first, I wanted to kill you," Jess said. "And James wanted to kill me. But once we talked it through, he understood. He's excited about the new baby, and even though I wasn't thinking we were ready for another one so soon, he's glad our children will be close in age the way he and Cole are. As for you..."

Jess looked at Allie with compassion. "Even without hearing how you came to tell Cole, I know you didn't mean to. I suspect it was something like how Cole ended up telling everyone else. You were thinking more about me, and it hadn't occurred to you until too late that you weren't supposed to tell. And, it was kind of my fault too. I should have told James. I put so much energy into worrying about how I could make it special for him that I forgot the joy of enjoying these precious stages of my pregnancy together."

Funny how in this discussion of the situation that would break most friendships, Jess was doing her best to properly assign blame. But maybe that's why they were such good friends.

"Thank you. I really am sorry. And I'm glad you're not pointing fingers and being ugly over everything. Over the past few days, I've realized just how crazy we all get with blaming each other and not taking responsibility for ourselves."

Over steaming cups of lavender tea, Allie told her friend about everything that had happened with her mother, Nadia, and Cole.

"How did you figure out who Nadia was and the reason she hated you?"

She shrugged. "It was the weirdest thing. I was praying about the situation because, until Gram confronted my mother, I'd completely forgotten about the affair. So, I asked God to reveal to me what I needed to know, and what my part in the situation was so I could make amends. I remembered seeing Nadia in the lunchroom at school, and she walked right up to me, told me I had ruined her life, dumped her lunch on me, and stormed off. I wanted to hide, which was what I was trying to do when Cole came up to me with a rag and tried to wipe off the food. He kept telling me to let him help, and I was crying, and I yelled at him to leave me alone because he was a creep."

Tears filled Allie's eyes as she remembered how ugly she'd been to him, when he'd just been trying to be nice. It wasn't even that he'd touched her inappropriately. He'd only gotten as far as brushing her shoulders with the rag.

"Over the years, I focused more on the incident of him

being creepy to me in the lunchroom than I did about what started it all. I was humiliated that day, but because I already hated him, I put all the blame on him. I started to realize that a lot of the things I hated him for were situations just like that."

Jess gave her a hug. "There were times when he legitimately embarrassed you. I can't imagine you did anything to make him think it was okay to sing to you at the homecoming rally."

"No way! I didn't want the flowers, the locker decorations, the weird ads in the school newspaper declaring his love for me. Trust me, there were a lot of things he did wrong. But I also didn't handle any of those situations as I should have. I should have just gone directly to him and said, 'Cole, even though I'm nice to you, it doesn't mean I like you. I will never be your girlfriend, and we're not even friends. So please, stop bothering me.'"

Jess laughed. "It is funny, with as blunt as your grandmother always is, how you can't seem to be."

The door opened, and James walked in with Cole behind him, looking thoughtful. The poor guy had probably witnessed way too much weird emotional girl stuff. But she had to give him credit for being a good sport and not running away screaming.

"I don't like hurting people's feelings. I've seen how Gram tends to hurt others with her direct speech. Granted, I'm used to it, and a lot of the time, it's pretty funny. But I know she's ruined a lot of relationships because she couldn't just keep her mouth shut."

Then Allie turned and smiled at the guys. "And speaking of keeping my mouth shut, I hope you know, James, that I am so sorry for how I ruined Jess's surprise."

James came over and gave her a quick hug. "All is

forgiven. Your heart was in the right place, as was my brother's. How can I fault you for that?"

"Good," she said. "And now, I promise, no more of this emotional stuff that I keep blathering on about. It's been a crazy season, but I don't need to drag everyone else into it."

The smile on Jess's face warmed her heart. "But that's what friends are for. And we're here for you, even in the crazy season. So seriously, tell us what we can do to help. What's the status on everything?"

She took a deep breath, wondering where to start. So much had gone on, it was hard to sift through all the information to determine what was and wasn't important. Especially because she wasn't sure herself. But as she sipped her lavender tea, feeling warm and comforted, that's where she began.

"It's hard to say. The insurance adjuster is still determining the amount of my claim, if any, that can be paid. There was a problem with my last insurance payment, and they haven't decided whether or not I fall into the grace period, or my coverage has lapsed."

Allie didn't want to mention the embarrassing part about the problem being her fault. She still didn't know what had happened to that payment, but obviously, she'd done something wrong that it hadn't gotten into the mail as it was supposed to.

But that didn't matter. Nor was it the only holdup. "They also have to do an investigation into the fire to rule out insurance fraud. Apparently, someone gave an anonymous tip telling them that I'd just lost my job and was short of money and that I'd mentioned hoping for a good insurance payout. The fact that it follows so closely on my car accident claim got them thinking perhaps my fire wasn't an accident."

She let out a long sigh. She didn't have any enemies, not really. Except for maybe Nadia, but she couldn't see even Nadia stooping that low.

"Since I obviously didn't set the fire, I know they will eventually find in my favor, but until then, everything is at a standstill. The insurance company won't pay out on my claim until the arson investigation is complete. Even when they don't suspect foul play, it usually takes several weeks to get the report."

Her friends murmured sympathetically. It was nice to feel like they were on her side, even if there wasn't anything they could do besides wait.

In the past, having Cole present what have made her feel jumpy. Now, it was a comfort to have him there. In just a few short weeks, he'd gone from being her enemy to someone she looked forward to seeing. Hopefully, he would choose to stay in Arcadia Valley, and they could further their friendship.

Except as she looked into his warm brown eyes, she wasn't sure that being his friend was enough anymore.

*Wait. What?*

*Am I actually attracted to him?*

She'd felt a twinge of something when they were talking to Kate outside the Gas N' Shop. Unlike the irritation she used to feel when people intimated there was something between her and Cole, she actually felt... Pride. That someone as loving and generous as Cole Anderson would be paired up with her. And when he'd been part of the denial, she had felt... Regret.

Maybe it was time she took a deeper look at him.

"What will you do in the meantime?" James asked. "Jess said that all of your supplies were in there as well. Do you have any products you can sell? Is there anything you can make?"

So many questions. Things Allie still needed to work out.

"Fortunately, I did have some products in the house, as well as some supplies I'd brought with me to Wade's. Initially, I was afraid I wouldn't be able to fill the orders I had, but Gram had stashed a bunch of products in her root cellar to make space in the house for all the wedding stuff. I just figured she'd put it all in the barn. Since she didn't, I can fill my present orders."

That small finding had been the first thing to give her hope. But there were other little miracles along the way.

"Even though the greenhouse fire killed most of my indoor plants, the plants I have in the fields are all right. Obviously, they won't be ready until summer. But when I moved into Wade's house, I brought a bunch of my plants with me. It was weird, living by myself for the first time, so I went a little overboard. I can use those plants to make some limited-edition products. My dad suggested I could advertise them as such, and charge a little bit more to make up for the fact that my production will be slowed until my next harvest."

Jess gave her a funny look. "Your dad?"

She nodded slowly. "That's right. I left out that part. Like I said, it's been a whirlwind."

She sat back in her chair and took another sip of her tea before continuing.

"Once all the bickering died down after the fire, Andrew and I sat with my business plan to see how we could adjust things. My dad and Uncle Stephen were hovering over our shoulders. At first, I thought they were being critical. But then they both started tossing out useful suggestions. For the first time in my life, they sounded like they were actually interested in what I was doing. It's still going to take a while to rebuild, but I feel good about where I'm headed."

The surprise on Jess's face made her smile. "I know. It's crazy. But Gram really told my parents off, and I think they actually listened for a change."

"Don't tell me your mother is being helpful, too."

She shook her head. "No. She didn't like me standing up to her, and she now hides from me whenever I'm at Gram's. It's still pretty tense over there, but at least people seem to have accepted that I'm going to carry on my lavender business no matter what."

The baby started fussing in the other room.

"I'll get her," Cole said.

It was sweet, watching him take over his niece's care. Most men were terrified of babies. But as he reentered the room, kissing Caitlin's chubby little cheeks, her heart melted.

She tried to catch his eye and smile at him, but just as she did so, he looked away. She'd noticed throughout the conversation that he hadn't been giving her direct eye contact.

Didn't that just figure that when she finally decided she might be attracted to him, he was acting completely uninterested?

Or maybe she'd overstayed her welcome.

"I should probably get going," she said. "I promised Gram I'd join them for a family dinner."

Jess stood and gave her another hug. "I'm glad we could finally catch up."

As she turned to leave, Jess said, "oh, wait. I have some stuff I have for you. Cole asked me to run it by, but I was feeling so terrible, I kept putting it off. And then I was going to give it to at the wedding, but we all know how nuts that was."

She left the room and returned, carrying a small box. "This is all of the stuff from your car. Cole was afraid, that with the window down, your papers would get ruined. So, he put it all in a box for me to bring to you. I'd forgotten until now. I'm sorry. I hope there was nothing important in there."

A sinking feeling hit her stomach as her gaze caught the envelopes at the top of the stack in the box.

The heat bill she'd been so desperate to pay. Based on that, she was pretty sure that every bill she'd needed to pay was there as well.

At least that was one more mystery solved.

"What's wrong?" Jess touched her arm, looking concerned.

"Nothing. I didn't know why all the bills I had didn't get paid when I was sure I had paid them. With the accident, I'd forgotten to go by the post office, but until now, I had no idea what happened to my payments."

"I hope they aren't too late," Jess said. "I'd feel terrible if you owed a bunch of fees because I couldn't get my act together and get you that box."

It didn't seem fair to tell Jess about all the troubles she'd had because of those missing envelopes. Especially when Cole gave her a knowing look.

In the past, she'd have been furious with him for taking her things out of her car without her permission. And she would've found a way to blame him for all the bad things that happened as result. But it wasn't his fault, any more than it was Jess's fault. Allie should have also remembered that she'd still had other errands to run.

"No, it's all right. Everything has worked out just fine."

And the truth was, it had. Since Hayden was a lawyer, he had already started looking into the legalities of the insurance company denying her claim while in her grace period. She'd already given the insurance company a new check. Wade had saved the day over their heat bill, and when she went back over her account, and realized all the checks that hadn't cleared, she stopped payment and sent new ones.

Mistakes happened, and they all had their own part. But she was learning you could let those mistakes be the end of the world, or you could fix them and move on. She thought that's what she'd always done, except now, she realized the blame game had played such a large role in her moving on that she hadn't really moved on.

She gave Jess another hug and returned to the farm.

Gram had the table spread out with leftovers from the dishes their friends in Arcadia Valley had brought over. It was sweet to see how many people had organized meals for the family, even though they were still technically capable of cooking for themselves. But as Gram's friend Mona said, it was one less thing for them to worry about. People had even been very conscientious about making sure Gram's dietary needs with her diabetes were appropriately met.

When Andrew came inside, Allie pointed to the box. "You'll never guess what I just found. All the missing bills? When my car was towed to the Andersons', Cole took all the papers out and put them in a box, thinking he was being helpful so they wouldn't get ruined by the elements. Jess was supposed to get the box to me, only she got busy, and it didn't work out."

"No way. At least we know what happened, even though we managed to get everything straightened out."

Allie grinned. "That's exactly what I told Jess."

"So, is this one more thing we're going to tar and feather

Cole Anderson for?" Caroline asked, reaching past her to grab some fresh vegetables from the veggie tray.

She shook her head, feeling a deep sense of peace in her heart. "No. It wasn't his fault. It's like I've learned recently. Sometimes things happen, and there are a lot of reasons why. We can spend all our time and energy being mad and blaming someone, or we can just move on. I'm choosing to move on. With everything."

She looked at her mother, who still hadn't apologized for their disagreement. It no longer mattered if she did or not.

"I know there's a lot of bad blood between us. And it doesn't matter to me who started it or why. I hope we can start again. But I'm done apologizing for being who I am."

Though she did not look impressed by Allie's words, the rest of the family nodded.

"I know that some of you think Gram is crazy. Dad, Uncle Stephen, Aunt Camille, and all the other aunts and uncles who couldn't come here. Wouldn't come here, because of whatever grudges they have. I hope you guys will go back to them and tell them that, whatever problems they have, they should just get over it or find a way to work things out. But we're all so busy being mad at each other and blaming each other for things that have a lot of causes."

Allie took a deep breath. She hadn't planned on doing this, but it seemed like the perfect time. She didn't even know how Gram was going to respond.

"I don't remember everything that happened because I was too young. But I know something in this family broke when Uncle Adam died. Gram and I have been talking about how much she misses him, and how she regrets not staying in touch with his widow and daughter. But I've been talking online with his daughter, Madison. She's married and has children, and I know that Gram would love to meet them. But her mother warned her about all the family drama, and she isn't sure she wants to be part of it."

The stunned expressions that crossed everyone's faces made it hard for her to decide if this was a happy surprise or a bad surprise. But at the tears in Gram's eyes, she knew she was doing the right thing.

"So maybe it's time we all figure out how to get over whatever we need to get over so Gram can finally meet Madison's children and catch up with the granddaughter she has missed so much. And maybe, if we can all find a way to get along, the next family wedding will have everyone here instead of people sending regrets and checks that don't replace human beings."

Layla came over to her and put her arm around her. "I am so blessed to have you as my sister-in-law."

Then Layla looked around the room. "Allie is right. I'm so grateful to have finally had the chance to get to know my Quintana relatives, and I know that Madison and her children will benefit from knowing you all, as well as the Bigbys who aren't here, if you're just willing to let go of your old grudges and prejudices."

Andrew joined them and gave Layla a kiss on top of her head. "And don't forget the joy you have in your newfound family now that you and your father have reconciled."

"I'm grateful for reconciliation, too," Caroline said, standing. "I still don't agree with everything my parents say, but I will never regret the time we took to work through our problems so they can fully be a part of my life now. Mom, Dad, Uncle Bart, Aunt Mary, you guys seem to be representing the rest of the family in the matter against Gram. You know she's not crazy, and you know we're not taking advantage of her. So why don't you talk to them and see what we can do to reconcile everyone to make the Bigby family whole again."

Hayden came to stand by his wife and hugged her to him. "As the lawyer originally hired by the family, I agree with everything that's been said. You all had your own negative views of Enid, but as we've spent time here together, it's really clear that we all have work to do on our relationships."

Having the support of her cousins and their spouses made her feel for the first time like she wasn't the screw-up Bigby. No, her life wasn't perfect, but she was figuring things out.

Gram stood and pointed a bony finger at her. "You've been praying those prayers like I told you to, haven't you?"

"I don't think I'd have been able to do any of this without them," she said honestly.

"Good," Gram said. "Then I can start working on knitting baby booties and hats. The way I figure, between you and the newlyweds, there's going to be a baby boom here real soon."

"You can leave me out of it," she said. "Not only am I not married, but I'm not dating anyone. It'll be a little hard for me to have a baby."

Everyone laughed except Gram. "It's going to happen sooner than you think, and in a most unexpected way."

## 16

Cole had spent the past several weeks avoiding Allie. Actually, he thought he was doing a pretty good job, considering the following week was Valentine's Day, and he'd gone past both Facets and Blossoms by the Akers without even taking a peek in the window.

All right, so maybe he had peeked. But that was ridiculous. He'd heard her flat out tell Jess that she had no feelings for him. The trouble was, knowing she had no feelings for him didn't change his feelings for her any more than it had in high school. The heart knows what it wants, or at least he remembered a saying to that effect. And what his heart wanted was Allie.

He walked into the church knowing he was supposed to give Uncle Vince an answer about taking on the worship pastor position permanently. But he didn't know. He had been enjoying the work, especially the music. When he played, even with the weight of Allie's eyes upon him, everything felt like it was exactly the way it was supposed to be.

The trouble was, he wasn't sure he would feel the same

way if she had a boyfriend or husband sitting next to her. When you loved someone, you were supposed to love them enough to want the best for them. Even though he'd prayed for God's best for her, and was prepared to accept her marrying someone else that God deemed a better match, he wasn't sure he could stick around to watch.

Fortunately, Uncle Vince wasn't in his office, buying him a little time. Maybe if he worked on some of the new music he was hoping to introduce to the congregation, it would help him gather his thoughts.

When he got into the music room, Enid Bigby was sitting there like she'd been there for a while, her knitting in hand.

"Enid! What a pleasant surprise. What brings you here? Is everything all right with Allie?" His heart sank as he realized that he shouldn't have asked that question. "I mean, is everything all right with the farm?"

Enid set her knitting down. "I know exactly what you meant. You love her, don't you?"

Everyone knew Enid Bigby was the biggest lie-detector in town. What must she think of him, still mooning over her granddaughter after all these years?

"Yes. But she doesn't return my feelings, and I don't want to make her the subject of unwanted attention. I've learned from my mistakes, and I care too much for her to hurt her again."

Enid made a noise as she stood. "You young people, fools that you are. Did she actually say to you that she doesn't love you?"

"She's too polite for that. That's always been her problem. Instead of confronting difficult situations or saying what's on her mind, she hides. But I overheard her telling Jess that she doesn't even like me. I don't want to make things any harder on her than they already are. I've done my best to stay out of her way and leave her alone. You should, too. She won't appreciate you interfering in her life like this."

It was too bad she couldn't hear him standing up for her. Would it matter to her at all to know how hard he was trying to do the right thing?

"That's what you get for avoiding her. If you'd spent time around her lately, you'd know she has no problem giving her opinion. That little spitfire is more opinionated than I am. She told off the whole family. On Skype."

Even though it sounded somewhat out of character for her, he could see it. After all, she'd bravely stood up to Nadia at the Gas N' Shop, trying to make peace with her.

"What changed?" he asked.

"She's been talking to God about things. You know, if you give God your heart and you talk to Him, and you promise to listen to what He says, you start doing the things you should be doing."

He shook his head. "Maybe that works for some people, but it hasn't been working for me. I keep praying about whether or not I should accept the full-time worship pastor position, but God has not made it clear to me."

"What has God been saying to you?" The way Enid looked at him with those beady eyes of hers made him squirm. Like she knew things about him she wasn't supposed to know.

And that was the trouble. God had been giving him direction, but following it meant breaking his promise to Allie.

"I keep getting the feeling I should talk to her. For some reason, I think talking to her would give me the clarity I need."

He'd had that feeling for some time now, but had been afraid to act on it because he didn't want to bother her.

"So why don't you? You young people, hearing from God and then not listening. Then you get all upset when God doesn't answer your other questions."

He chuckled softly. "And you've done a perfect job, listening to God?"

"No." Enid smacked her hand on the table. "That's why I'm telling you to. Learn from my mistakes. Go talk to her. You can even tell her that I sent you. She doesn't argue if it's an order from me."

This time, Cole didn't bother trying to control his laughter. As much as he hated to admit it, Enid's orders trumped anything anybody else might want. She was a force to be reckoned with, and even though a lot of people still thought she was crazy, no one was crazy enough to cross her.

"So, you think I should just walk up to her and tell her that God's been telling me to talk to her about my future? And she should listen to me because you said it was okay?"

"No, you amateur." Enid made a disgusted noise. "You don't just go to someone and tell them God told you to do something. That's how you get labeled crazy. I should know. What you have to do is come up with a good excuse for talking to her."

This was entirely unhelpful. "No offense, but I've been down that road before. I'm shocked I didn't get labeled a stalker because of it."

"That's because you lacked finesse and a firm conviction. You might have thought you had one but, back then, it was just wishful thinking. But now, I see the way the two of you have interacted, the maturity, and the mutual respect based on something other than the fact that Allie has a cute butt."

He opened his mouth to disagree about Allie's butt, and

then realized he couldn't honestly argue against it being cute. However, that was never fully the reason why he liked her.

"Ever since I was a kid, I cared about Allie because she was the nicest person I knew."

Enid looked unimpressed. "But she hadn't found her backbone yet. She was too nice. Which is why you got strung along for so long. Now, she knows who she is and what she wants. And any fool can see that she wants you."

Now that was some wishful thinking.

"Has she told you that?"

A wicked grin filled Enid's face.

"No, but I know her better than you do. And she looks at you the way she looks at cupcakes. She knows she's not supposed to have them, too much sugar and all that garbage. But one day, I fully expect to see her in a bathtub full of them because she likes them so much."

Somehow, that image just seemed gross to Cole. But from Enid's gleeful expression, it apparently meant something really good.

"I'll take your word for it. So, seriously, what next?"

Uncle Vince walked into the music room.

"Pastor! I see you got my message," Enid said. "I'm not one to ask for charity for myself. But that insurance company is still fighting Allie on paying her claim for the barn and greenhouse. She's been a big part of our community, and you know she'll help anyone she can."

Emily, the woman Cole remembered from the ER whose children Allie had taken home with her on Christmas, entered the room. Uncle Vince had given her a job working in the church office when he found out about her situation.

"Just look at Emily," Enid said. "Emily, how much has Allie helped you?"

"A lot." She looked confused. "Please don't tell me that you sent an urgent message for me to come here to ask me that question. You shouldn't have to. Thanks to Allie, I'm going to church now. And I have this job. What's going on?"

Enid smiled, and Cole knew that she already had a plan. She was just setting everyone up to be part of it.

"As I said, the insurance company still has not determined the cause of the fire, and therefore has not given her any money to rebuild her greenhouse. I found out that Allie has a wonderful opportunity to have her products distributed so more people can experience them. However, without her greenhouse and production space, she won't be able to enter the partnership according to the timeline set out."

The look Enid gave him told Cole that the next part was going to be a big ask. And it was all going to be about him.

"So, I want you to put on a benefit concert for Allie. We'll have it in our main barn, the one not damaged by the fire. People will buy tickets, and all the money will go to rebuilding the greenhouse."

Cole stared at her. On the one hand, he'd be happy to do that for Allie. On the other hand, his past actions were against him. "You know about homecoming my senior year, right?"

Enid snorted. "Please. Everyone knows that story. You were just ahead of your time. Now kids do these crazy proposal-type things to ask each other to dances, and it's a big production. It's expected. She should have said yes instead of sitting at home, moping about the bozo who didn't ask her."

That still didn't give him a lot of confidence about putting on a concert for Allie.

"I'd feel better about it if you asked her permission."

"I told you, she doesn't say no to me. She might want to, but she still has respect for her elders."

Everyone except Enid chuckled.

"What do you need from me?" Uncle Vince asked.

"I just want your blessing to have it in the church bulletin and to pass out flyers here. And I'll be expecting you and the missus to attend. I can count on you for two tickets, right?"

Uncle Vince shook his head as he laughed. "Of course, you can. How much are the tickets?"

"Twenty dollars each. There will also be baskets for people to bid on. The Grannies and I will be talking to local businesses for basket donations and to put up flyers. If we raise more money than what Allie needs, or the insurance comes through, then you can help us figure out a worthy cause to donate the extra funds to."

Enid looked like she had it all figured out and wasn't going to accept no for an answer.

"And me?" Emily asked. "What's my role in this?"

"I'm too old for this tomfoolery. This might be my idea, but I need younger bones to make it happen. The Grannies and I will help, but I want you to coordinate it all."

As much as he wanted to say yes, part of him was terrified that Allie was going to kill them. Not only did she not like being the center of attention, she also tended to shy away from people doing things for her.

Emily didn't seem to have the same hesitation. "Of course, I will. I love planning events. It's been my favorite part of working in the church."

The door opened, and Agnes walked in. He looked over at Uncle Vince, who looked just as surprised as he was.

"It's about time you showed up," Enid said. "Cole has been having his doubts about taking the job, and I'm pretty sure I'm going to have to strong-arm him into doing the benefit for Allie."

Cole went over to the old woman and gave her a big hug. "It is so good to see you. How are you?"

"Dying, but we all are. Just some of us sooner than others." She squeezed him tight. "I have a little life left in me, hopefully a lot, but only the good Lord knows how much. The warm air in California during my treatment felt good, and Jerry and I have decided to move there. But first, I want to sing one last song with you. And we're going to do it at Allie's concert."

There was no way he could say no now. But he suspected that Enid knew that. She grinned like the Cheshire Cat as she looked over at Uncle Vince.

"He hasn't said it yet, and he doesn't think he's sure yet. But this nephew of yours will be our new worship pastor. Also, you'll be doing a wedding for him and Allie. This time, I don't want any of that solemn nonsense. For their wedding, I expect you to smile a little more than you did for Andrew's. You speak in the same monotone when you're preaching at a wedding as you do at a funeral. We're going to work on that."

Cole just shook his head slowly. "Don't you think Allie should have something to say about all of this? She's already said that she doesn't want a big wedding."

Unfortunately, defending her only made Enid's grin wider. "You let me worry about that," she said.

He would try. But he was also going to spend a lot more time in prayer over the situation. The last thing he needed was for all of this to backfire and for Allie to hate them all.

## 17

Allie was going to kill her grandmother. Forget everything she'd been saying about family unity. And the fact that she had spent the past year or so trying to save the woman's life. She'd been on Gram's side all this time. But with this stunt, that crazy old lady had gone too far.

The trouble was, she'd had nearly a month to get Gram to see reason. And so far, nothing had worked. Every time she tried to talk to her, Gram had urgent business elsewhere. Even Cole, who had already been avoiding her, was like a ghost. There was evidence he existed, but seeing him for herself seemed next to impossible.

Even worse, how was she supposed to argue over everyone being so nice to her? Every business in Arcadia Valley had donated a gift certificate or basket or something as part of the silent auction. Gram was busy arguing with the fire department over how many chairs they could get in the barn and still meet fire code, because apparently, they sold that many tickets.

Nice problem to have, she supposed, but it felt like an

enormous amount of pressure to have all these people paying good money to support her business. Her barn had burned down. What made them think their money wouldn't go to waste?

She sighed as she went inside Gram's house to get her remaining product. She'd branded it as a special edition, just like her father had said, and she had almost sold out of all of it as well. Gram told her she needed to have the rest of it for sale at the benefit in case people wanted some.

Even though she had a million other things to do to get ready for the evening, Allie couldn't help making herself a cup of lavender tea.

As she sat steeping her tea, she prayed that God would help her through the situation. It was so weird to ask about something that seemed like a gift from God, yet she didn't feel right accepting it.

The door opened, and Cole entered. "Allie. I'm glad I caught you. It's been crazy the past few weeks, and we haven't had a chance to talk."

He shook his head. "No, that's not true. I've been avoiding you. I know I promised there would be no more stunts, and I wouldn't try helping you out without your permission. I just wanted you to know that the only reason I'm doing this is because your grandmother asked me to. I'm sure you know how difficult it is to tell her no."

The expression on his face twisted her heart in a funny way. It was sweet to see how deeply torn he was at the idea of breaking his promise to her.

"Don't worry, I understand," she said. "I can't tell you how many times I've opened my mouth to ask her to stop this crazy thing, but no words came out. Gram's heart is in the right place, and I only hope I can live up to the faith everyone has in me."

He looked surprised for a moment, then he nodded. "I was pretty sure you'd hate the idea. But I don't know what you mean about living up to the faith people have in you."

She let out a long sigh. "I'm not exactly the poster child for successful businesswomen. So much of what has happened has been because of my irresponsibility. And yet, here are all these people, donating their time and money to help me rebuild when there's no guarantee I'm going to make a success of it."

"I believe in you." The look in his eyes almost made her want to believe in herself too. It reminded her a lot of Gram, Andrew, and Caroline, and how they always encouraged her in all of her ideas. Except there was also something more. He wasn't saying it because he loved her and automatically believed in her, but because there was something he legitimately saw in her.

It was so strange, seeing that expression on his face. Mostly because as she'd gotten to know him over the past few months, she'd realized there was a lot to like about Cole Anderson. And now, she liked him even more.

Actually, she more than liked him. It was hard not to, with the way he always seemed to care about others. And here he was, encouraging her once more.

"But why?" she asked. "How do you even know what you're believing in? With the way you've been avoiding me, you don't even know my plans."

The sheepish look on his face made her wish she could reach out and give him a big hug. Why did things always have to feel so awkward between them?

"I told you I wasn't going to push myself on you. You don't like me. I get it. Given all our mutual connections, I know you would have been polite now that we've cleared the air between us. But I couldn't bear the thought of bothering you anymore. It's just not worth it to make you uncomfortable."

She stared at him. "What do you mean, I don't like you? Of course, I like you. I thought we'd worked all that out. I thought we'd reached a point of connection."

But she'd already convinced herself that perhaps she was mistaken.

"You don't have to be polite. Not with me anymore. The day you found out it was my fault your bills didn't get paid on time, I overheard you tell Jess you don't like me. And that was before you realized I almost ruined your chances at getting an insurance payout."

It took her a moment to think about what he could have possibly misinterpreted. "I wish you'd asked me about it. You missed the part where I told Jess that's what I wish I'd have said to you back in high school, so there weren't so many misunderstandings between us. I've actually come to like you a lot. But maybe it's better I didn't let you know my real feelings for you. We're still stuck in this old pattern of misunderstandings, and I want a relationship with someone who's willing to learn and grow and talk things out with me."

As she explained her side of things, she realized that perhaps she was being a little too hasty in writing off the potential of a relationship with him because they were doing the "talking out" part right then.

Were they in a relationship?

It seemed like it in some ways, especially because they'd worked through so much. But was it enough?

He stared at her. "You have feelings for me?"

"Let's not say that too loudly, because the next thing you know, Gram is going to be planning a wedding and Jess will be right there with her."

"Would that be so bad? Or do you have feelings, but not in that way?"

She looked down at her teacup, knowing that the answers were not swirling somewhere in the water, but needing that time to figure out what her feelings were. If they were clearing the air, the way she had said she wanted to, then she needed to be clear on what she wanted.

She finally returned her gaze to him. "It's a little weird to talk about a wedding when we haven't even been on a date."

"Would you be my date for your benefit?"

"I think that's the first time you actually asked me out to my face without some kind of crazy song and dance."

He laughed. "Is that a yes?"

"Yes." She smiled at him. "Even though I'm still mad at you for wasting all this time we could have already been dating."

He held out his hand to her. "But do I get a little credit for the fact that I was trying to respect you and your wishes?"

"Only if you're willing to admit that you made some incorrect assumptions." She took his hand and winked.

He grinned. "If I do, do I get a kiss?"

"We haven't even gone on our first date, and you're already asking for a kiss?" She kept her tone light and teasing as he pulled her close.

"Honestly? If I thought you'd say yes, I'd ask you to marry me. I've loved you since third grade, and that's never changed."

She wasn't sure he was serious, at least not until she looked into his eyes. "You've always been in love with a vision of me. You haven't known the real me until very recently. Maybe you should slow it down and figure that out."

He brought her hand to his lips and kissed it.

"I've always known the real you. Maybe I misinterpreted a few things, but I know the person you've always been when people aren't looking. You're the woman who works every holiday so others get time off. You were the kid who shared her lunch with others who didn't have anything, even though you didn't have much either. You hid from a well-meaning but irritating dork who chased after you with bold declarations of love because you didn't want to hurt his feelings by outright rejecting him."

The way he talked about her, she would almost be in love with herself. "You just caught me on a few good days."

"And that's one more reason why I've always loved you, and why I always will. Because you never puff up yourself and act like you're better than everyone else. A lot of people would look at this benefit and think of it as something owed to them. But you, you're still wondering if you're worthy of so much generosity."

Her eyes filled with tears as she saw the sincerity on his face. Physical touch had always been awkward between them, but she fell into his arms and hugged him like it was the most natural place to be. He kissed the top of her head.

"You are so worthy, and you and your dreams mean so much to this community. And I hope you let me remain by your side to support you in that pursuit."

It felt so good being his arms that she had to wonder if the reason she'd avoided it for so long was that she wasn't sure she'd ever be able to leave.

"But what about you? What about your dreams? You came here to figure out what you were going to do with your life now that your plans were ruined. It might seem impossible now, but what happens when supporting me isn't enough for you?"

He pulled away slightly, so she could see him looking at her.

"I took your advice, and I've been praying about it. Arcadia Valley is my home and the thought of leaving, especially now that my brother has children, has been heartbreaking. Being the worship pastor at Arcadia Valley Community Church has been more rewarding than I thought. The only reason I'd considered leaving is because I couldn't bear looking out into the congregation and seeing you with someone else."

An expression of peace filled his face, and she knew that whatever conclusion he'd come to had been because of his time with God.

"I prayed that God would help me with those feelings, because I know that when you love someone, you want the best for them. And I do. If God has some other man for you, then I want you to be with him. But selfishly, I wanted it to be me. Today's conversation has given me a level of hope that I didn't think I dared have."

Nor had she. Which was weird, considering all the feelings he'd declared for her over the years. But it hadn't been until now that they'd both reached a level of maturity in their emotional states and in their relationships with God.

"So, you mentioned feelings for me," he said. "Are those the kind of feelings worth pursuing in a committed relationship? Or do you see me as some kind of high-level buddy?"

It was a fair question, but a noise outside the window caught her attention. People were arriving for the benefit, and they didn't have much longer to talk.

"I don't know if there's enough time for me to give you a proper answer. I can't believe Gram hasn't already started banging down the door, wondering where we are."

He shook his head slowly, smiling. "You think maybe she

might have had a hand in us having this much time together alone?"

Though she hadn't considered until now, it made perfect sense. And once again, she couldn't help chuckling to herself at how handily Gram had arranged everything.

"You're going to make me say it, aren't you?"

It was weird, considering she hadn't fully admitted it to herself. Except deep in her heart, she knew it was true.

"You were the one who wanted honesty and openness between us."

She nodded and took a deep breath as she said a final prayer that the right words would come. "I'm in love with you."

A strange look crossed his face. He closed his eyes. And for a moment, Allie thought he might even keel over. But then he looked at her.

"As many times as I've imagined you saying that to me, it never felt as good as it does now. Will you say it to me often?"

The little boy he'd once been peeked out for a moment, and she wanted to hold him and tell him that yes, she really did love him, and the more she thought about it, the more it was true. Except someone started banging on the back door.

"Hurry up in there," Gram said. "We have a benefit ready to begin, and our guest of honor and entertainment are missing. So, admit you're in love with each other, kiss, and let's get on with the show."

Allie couldn't help laughing. "You were right about Gram. I guess I better let you kiss me now."

"Nope. Our first kiss isn't going to be something I rush. You've kept me waiting all these years, we can wait until after the benefit. And then you'd better be prepared for a whole lot of kissing."

She smiled as they walked out of the house, hand-in-hand. A few months before, the idea of kissing Cole Anderson was about the most disgusting ever. And now, she had butterflies dancing in her stomach at the thought of his promise of a whole lot of kissing.

The concert began as scheduled, and while she enjoyed the music, what she enjoyed more was all the encouraging glances and smiles people gave her. These were her people, and this was her home. As much as she'd always labeled herself a screw-up, they obviously didn't see her that way. It was as Cole said they saw something special in her.

She glanced to the other side of the barn, where her mother sat with her father, looking extremely put out. But it didn't bother her anymore. Whatever her mother's issue was, it was her issue. She had done her part, and that was enough for both Allie and God.

Turning her attention back to the stage, she saw that Cole was finishing one of the new worship songs they'd started singing at church. Agnes had joined him as a final farewell before she and her husband moved to California. Allie liked the new direction the music was taking, a mix of the traditions Agnes had started and a few new surprises along the way, like the song Cole had just sung.

As the applause died down, Cole turned his gaze on Allie. A spotlight came up on them both.

"I'm sure you've all heard different versions of the stories of the crazy things I did to get Allie's attention back in high school. And I kind of promised her I wasn't going to do any of that again. But you see, she told me she loved me today, and I think you all know I love her too."

On the other side of her, Gram leaned in to her and whispered, "I knew it."

She elbowed Gram. "Shh."

Being in the spotlight was definitely not fun, but she at least wanted to hear what he had to say.

"The first time I sang to her, it was a very unoriginal knockoff from a movie. But if you'll all indulge me, I'd like to sing a song I spent my whole life writing for the girl I've spent my whole life loving, and if she'll have me, the girl I intend to keep loving forever."

All eyes were on her, and he sang, reflecting the words he'd just spoken.

Gram leaned into her again. "I told him to sing you a song, but this is way better than what I had in mind."

This time, Allie gave her a harder poke.

He kept singing, promising her a life of love, support, and working together to make their dreams come true. Tears streamed down her face as she realized that he had already kept all the promises he was making her in the song.

When the music ended, he took off his guitar and walked off stage toward her. "I didn't plan this part, but after what we talked about in the kitchen, and being reminded of how God has already worked in our lives, I just know this is something I've got to do."

She didn't have to hear his next words to know what was coming. And it didn't require more than the briefest of prayers to know her answer.

"Will you marry me?" he asked, getting down on one knee. "I didn't have time to go by Facets, but I did find a few stray pieces of lavender I fashioned into something that'll have to do until we can choose something together."

The ring he held up had indeed been made from strands of lavender he'd somehow woven together to make a ring.

"Yes," she said, smiling as he slipped it onto her finger. She reached forward to kiss him, but he pulled her into a hug instead.

"Later," he whispered. "I told you I wanted our first kiss to be special, and that is not going to happen with an audience."

She grinned. "Just don't make me wait too long."

Everyone in the barn applauded, and from somewhere in the back, someone yelled, "Well that went a whole lot better than homecoming."

They joined hands, and Cole held them up, showing off her makeshift engagement ring. "It sure did," he said. "And she's not even crying this time."

Except she was. But those were happy tears, and as friends and family rushed to congratulate her, she didn't feel like running away because he'd tried to woo her with a song. Although, she really did hope that they could leave soon, because she was eager to kiss her future groom.

# EPILOGUE

When they broke ground on Allie's new greenhouse, she didn't feel the panic she used to feel at the thought of doing anything to expand her lavender business. With Cole by her side, she felt strong and confident.

The insurance had finally paid on her claim, giving her the needed funds to rebuild. Her benefit had also raised more money than she would have ever imagined. When she had found out the insurance was going to pay after all, she'd tried to let people know she wanted to return their money, but no one would let her. Apparently, they hadn't forgotten about all the times she'd let folks go without paying, and since all of her records of who owed what had been destroyed in the fire, they said it evened the account.

Which it didn't, because they'd raised way more than people owed her, but Cole had told her to stop arguing.

So here they were, on this gorgeous June day, breaking ground. She'd started new plants inside the house she was renting from Wade, and she'd had enough to transplant into little pots to give everyone as thank-you gifts.

It wasn't nearly enough to express her appreciation for how much she loved the people in Arcadia Valley, but since lavender had given her so much comfort and love over the years, she prayed it would do the same for them.

As she handed out the last plant, Cole came over and put his arm around her. "You did a fantastic job. We're going to have re-name Arcadia Valley, Lavender Valley, with all the plants that will be growing around this town."

"Shh... don't give away my evil plan." She looked up at him and grinned, then he bent and gave her a quick kiss.

"Good! I hope this means you two are moving things along." Gram came up to them, holding up her knitting bag. "I just finished my third set of hats and booties, and there are no babies to fill them yet."

Allie tried not to groan, but Cole's nudge told her she'd failed.

"Babies will come when they come. Caroline and Hayden haven't been married a year, and Andrew and Layla are waiting until Andrew is done with school."

Gram gave her an eagle-eyed glare. "So, what's your holdup?"

"We have to have a wedding before there's a baby," Allie said, shaking her head.

Usually, that was enough to stop Gram in her tracks. Instead, Gram turned her gaze on Cole. "Well, why haven't you married her yet? You were speedy enough on the proposal."

He looked down at her with such a loving gaze, she almost would have married him on the spot.

"I have waited my whole life to marry her. A few more months won't kill us."

Gram snorted. "But it might kill me. Everyone's already

here. You ought to just get married and get it over with. Then you can start making some babies for me."

The only reason Allie was certain she wasn't going to die of mortification was that with all of Gram's other stunts over the years, she hadn't died yet. And this was by far one of Gram's tamer moments.

Cole drew Allie close. "Let's get one thing straight, Enid Bigby. You might get away with bossing people around over most things, and your orders definitely had a part in bringing us together. But our marriage, and our children, those aren't yours to dictate."

No one talked to Gram like that. Not even Layla, who had gotten pretty good at bending Gram to her will for medical reasons. And yet...

Gram grinned. "And that's why I brought you together. All right then, you do what you want. Fortunately, Madison is coming to visit soon, and bringing her children. They might not be babies, but at least someone's given me great-grandchildren."

As Cole gave Allie another squeeze, Gram stomped off.

He bent and gave her a nuzzle. "She's right, you know."

"About what?"

He turned so he was facing her. "Everyone *is* already here. We could get Uncle Vince to marry us right now."

"But we don't have a marriage license or anything." Allie looked around. It would be nice to have a wedding without a bunch of hassle.

"The courthouse is fifteen minutes away. If we tell your grandmother what we're up to, she can rally the Grannies to create a distraction to keep everyone here long enough for us to get the paperwork. It'll be a surprise until we actually have the ceremony."

His plan was almost brilliant.

"Gram is going to think we did this because she said so."

Cole bent and kissed her. "Let an old woman be happy."

And so, they did.

# COMING NEXT IN ARCADIA VALLEY

About the Book

When cookbook author and media personality Olivia Jennings suffers the biggest humiliation of her life on national TV, she thinks things can't get any worse... and then she promptly gets fired from the only thing she has left — her dream job. She hesitantly returns to her hometown of Arcadia Valley to heal her wounded pride and lean on her family in her time of crisis.

Wyatt Mason only ever wanted to do one thing: run his family's cattle ranch. In fact, the hardest time in Wyatt's life was the four years when his dad forced him to go off to college. His devotion to ranch life even ended his only serious relationship — his college sweetheart ended their engagement because she wasn't cut out for life on a cattle ranch. After some tough years, Wyatt will do whatever it takes to keep the family business afloat, even if it means stepping out of his comfort zone.

When Olivia and Wyatt are forced to team up for a project meant to relaunch her career and save his family's ranch, they immediately find themselves at odds. Wyatt is the kind of man Olivia has taken great pains to avoid — the kind who'd rather ride a horse than drive a sports car. And Olivia's high heels and perfect makeup prompt Wyatt to put her in the same category as his ex — way too prissy for ranch life. Can Olivia and Wyatt ever find common ground? If they can put their preconceived notions aside, they may have the perfect recipe for romance.

## SNEAK PEEK

A Recipe for Romance by Annalisa Daughety

*Grandma Jennings' homemade chocolate cake might not heal a broken heart, but it will at least take the sting away for a little while. —A Recipe for Every Occasion: A Modern Girl's Go To Cookbook.*

"These are the worst times of my life." Olivia Jennings gripped the plush leopard print blanket and pulled it over her head. "Turn off the TV, please. I'm tired of seeing my face." She curled up in a ball and wished she had a time machine. And better decision-making abilities. Olivia jumped when the blanket was suddenly snatched away.

She looked up with a scowl at the cover stealer. "It's not fair."

Brooke Lockwood tossed the cover at her sister. "Dramatic, much?" She clicked the TV off and sat down on the bed next to Olivia. She reached over and patted her on the arm. "It's not as bad as you think."

"No, it's not." Olivia reached for the cover again. "It's worse."

Brooke grabbed the blanket and held it out of Olivia's reach. "Nothing you can't get through. Jennings women are stronger than that."

Olivia felt a pang of shame. Her troubles were nothing compared to the things her older sister had dealt with over the past few years, losing her husband just before she was set to give birth to their first child. Now Brooke was a widow with a toddler. "I guess."

"Want to talk about it yet?"

Olivia shook her head. She'd kept most of the details of her recent stint on a reality TV show a secret. Her sisters only knew that it hadn't gone well. "What was I thinking?"

Riley Jennings walked into the bedroom in time to hear Olivia's question. "I believe your justification to us when we tried to talk you out of it was that competing on national TV for the love of a hunky weatherman would somehow boost your media career and help you sell more cookbooks."

Olivia frowned. "I'm pretty sure the opposite may be the case."

Riley sank into the recliner next to the bed. "Blake just left. We watched the first episode and thought it seemed to go well. In fact, I even mentioned to him that I thought there was a spark between you and Austin Granger. Or maybe that was just some kind of TV magic."

"There was a spark." Olivia really didn't want to relive the last three months, but seeing how her failed relationship would be playing out in living rooms across America for the next several weeks, maybe she should at least come clean to her sisters. "I knew him before I auditioned for the show. We worked at the same network for a short time." Olivia was a morning show host for a syndicated television show based out of New York. She'd recently started to fill in from time to time on one of the bigger morning shows, and had thought it might be her big break.

"That's right," Brooke said. "Didn't you two even do a few appearances together?"

Olivia nodded. "Yeah. We weren't really friends or anything, but at least he knew who I was."

Riley rolled her eyes. "Well why wouldn't he? Your cookbooks have done well and those cooking segments you do are great. Don't sell yourself short—you brought as much to the table as he did. More, if you ask me."

Olivia couldn't help but smile at her younger sister. "When did you get all wise and stuff?"

"She grew up while you were off chasing your dreams," Brooke said, matter-of-factly.

"I guess so." Olivia picked at the chipped polish on her nails. It had been eons since she'd had a proper manicure. "Anyway, I kind of think—at least I hope—that these first few episodes won't be too mortifying."

"So, it's not a stretch to guess that he didn't pick you in the end, right?" Riley asked.

Olivia made a face at her sister. "I'm under contract not to talk about that stuff. I'm not supposed to tell how long I lasted on the show or what happened in the end."

"Well we pretty much know that you stayed on till at least near the end," Brooke said. "We know how long filming took place and we know when you were back in New York."

But they didn't know what had happened when she'd returned to the city. "I can trust that you guys won't tell anyone this," she began. "And I've been warned that as the show continues to air, media may come here and start asking questions. So, you have to stay quiet." She looked from one sister to the other.

Brooke and Riley nodded silently.

"I was one of the final two women."

"I knew it!" Riley exclaimed. "I knew you'd make it till the end." Her grin faded quickly as Olivia shot her a look.

"That makes it harder, though, doesn't it?" Brooke asked quietly. "Because if you were in the final two, that means you had feelings for him."

"You came home because your heart is broken." Riley reached over and put her hand on top of Olivia's. "Is that why you're back in Arcadia Valley?"

If only it were that simple.

————

Wyatt Mason peered at the spreadsheet on his laptop and shook his head. The past couple of months had been tough for Mason Farms. He was already filled with dread at the thought of having to break the news to his dad.

"Here she is!" his niece, Jasmine, shrieked from her spot next to him on the couch. "Mom! Come in here."

Ever since his sister, Holly, and her thirteen-year-old daughter had moved in with his parents, things had been much livelier than Wyatt was used to. And much louder.

Holly stepped into the living room. "You aren't bothering your uncle Wyatt are you? He's trying to work." Her disapproving look was flashed in Wyatt's direction though, and not her daughter's. She'd been after Wyatt for weeks to leave work behind at night and learn to relax.

"But it's *Happily Ever After*," Jasmine explained. "You said there was a girl on there that you went to high school with."

Holly laughed. "No. I said there was a girl on there who went to the same high school as me. She was several years younger than me." She motioned for her daughter to scoot and plopped down next to her. "I know her family though."

Wyatt rolled his eyes. A reality show of all things. "I can feel my brain cells dying already. Don't you ever watch the news or something?"

Jasmine poked him in the arm. "Come on, Uncle Wyatt. This is like the number one show in the country. Don't you at least think Olivia Jennings is pretty?"

He looked up at the screen. Jasmine had paused the show and the blond woman smiling on the screen seemed vaguely familiar. "Who did you say she was?"

Holly picked up the remoted and hit the PLAY button. "Olivia Jennings. Her mom taught at the elementary school. There was a big thing on her in the newspaper a while back. She's written several cookbooks and was on a morning TV show where she demonstrated her recipes. She has a couple of sisters, too."

Wyatt thought back. "She's Katie Groves' cousin, isn't she?" He'd worked for Katie's dad when he was in junior high and vaguely remembered the group of giggling girls coming through the farmers market.

Holly laughed. "She goes by Kate now that she's a grown up. And it's Kate Harrison. She married Drew Harrison over the summer."

"The guy who runs the renovation business." Wyatt nodded his head as he said it. He knew Drew. "And Kate runs the Arcadia Valley Farmers Market now."

"Exactly," Holly said. "In fact, I'm pretty sure Dad's been trying to get you to go meet with her to see if there's room for a Mason Farms booth for next Spring."

Wyatt frowned. He and his dad didn't see eye-to-eye on

the best way to run the business. "Yeah, I've been putting it off."

"Don't put off till tomorrow what you can do today. Right, Mom?" Jasmine piped up.

Holly winked at her brother's scowl. "Right."

"Oh, she's so pretty," Jasmine said, as Olivia came back on the screen. "I wonder how she gets her hair to stay so perfectly waved like that."

Wyatt snorted. "That's probably her only hobby. She might've grown up in Arcadia Valley, but I'll bet she doesn't live around here now." He cast another glance at the screen. Olivia smiled at something the man next to her said, a picture-perfect smile. The man threw his head back and laughed, captivated by her charms. "If the chump knows what's good for him, he'll leave her alone," Wyatt said. "A girl like that will only break his heart."

Find more details at: http://arcadiavalleyromance.com/books/a-recipe-for-romance/

# THE ARCADIA VALLEY ROMANCE SERIES

# ABOUT THE AUTHOR

A self-professed crazy chicken lady, Danica Favorite loves the adventure of living a creative life. She and her family recently moved in to their dream home in the mountains above Denver, Colorado. Danica loves to explore the depths of human nature and follow people on the journey to happily ever after. Though the journey is often bumpy, those bumps are what refine imperfect characters as they live the life God created them for. Oops, that just spoiled the ending of all of Danica's stories. Then again, getting there is all the fun.

Subscribe to Danica's newsletter for all her latest news: http://eepurl.com/7HCXj

You can connect with Danica at the following places:

Amazon BookBub Instagram

www.danicafavorite.com/

# READER LETTER

Dear Reader,

I'm always amazed at the unexpected things that pop up when I write a book. I had a lot of fun with Allie's past because it brought me back to some of my own high school adventures. Hint: a lot of the ways Cole tortured her happened to me or one of my friends. And yes, I changed a few details to protect the innocent. But trust me, being serenaded in the middle of school in front of everyone is really embarrassing to a high school girl. Or at least it was to me.

Moments like that shape how we view ourselves and others. Poor Cole just wanted to show Allie how much he liked her, and Allie just wanted to be left alone. It took a lot of work for them to finally understand how the other person might feel and to act in a way that honored the other person.

I'm deeply troubled by a lot of things happening in the world right now. One of my quests over the past few months has been trying to understand my so-called enemies. Why would someone believe something I think is terrible? Why would someone do something I think is wrong? We live in a broken world, and like Enid taught Allie, I'm trying to do a better job of praying for my enemies and finding a compassionate lens through which to view them. I don't do it perfectly, but the more I try to share love and compassion, the more I realize how desperately our world needs it right now.

My hope for you is that you'll take the time to share love and compassion to your enemies as well. Maybe you don't have a nemesis from high school the way Allie did, but you never know when your worst enemy will be the person you need the most.

Thanks for reading, and as always, thank you for your support.

Danica Favorite